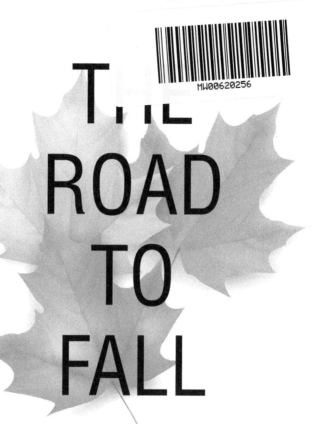

THE
ROAD
TO
FALL

ERIKA MORSE

THE
ROAD
TO
FALL

CHAPTER ONE

I SHOULD HAVE KNOWN WHAT I HAD GOTTEN MYSELF into. I cringed at Bobby's request and knew my reaction to it would change my future.

"Show me your boobs!" Bobby said as he leaned against my door with his arms crossed.

"Are you crazy? I'm not showing you my boobs! And what are you doing with my diary?" I asked with my hands on my hips.

Bobby smirked. "Okay. Then I guess I will have to tell everyone who your crush is. Let's see, Facebook or Snapchat? Evan, huh?"

"Wait!" I yelled. "Please don't. Here." I lifted my shirt and showed him my bra.

"Oh no, Olivia, I said your boobs. Not your bra."

My face turned red. I couldn't believe this.

"Bobby, I'm not showing you my boobs. Come on. Just forget this, please."

"Olivia, either show your tits or I tell. It's your choice."

I was shaking and couldn't believe what I was going to do, but I didn't want Evan to know; I would be humiliated. I unhooked my bra and quickly lifted it.

"I see puberty has not blessed you yet, Olivia. Thanks though." He opened my door and left.

I was humiliated and began to cry immediately, my self-confidence disappearing with every tear that fell. I was sure life as I knew it had just changed forever.

Even though my parents were having a dinner party downstairs, I couldn't bring myself to go back down, so I remained in my room agonizing about what had happened. I heard people leaving around nine, and when my mom came in to check on me, I pretended to be asleep.

The next morning the pit in my stomach was still present. I was silent on the way to school.

I was 13 and a freshman at Torrey Pines High School in San Diego, CA. Bobby was 16 and a junior. I really hoped I would not see him. He was really popular, tall, dark brown hair, and dark brown eyes to match. He was still holding onto his tan from the summer. He was beautiful. His best friend was Evan who was equally gorgeous and the one that I was crushing on.

The next morning as I walked into the school people were staring at me. There were a bunch of papers on the ground and taped to lockers. I leaned down to pick up the paper. The pit in my stomach became much bigger as I read: "Olivia Johnson is crushing on Evan Porter. Maybe she will show him her boobs just like she showed me last night!"

Just then Stacy, the meanest girl in school, pranced up to me. She had an evil smile on her face and while holding the flyer chided. "Gosh, Olivia, I had no idea that you were *that kind of girl*. I guess I better be careful that you don't try showing your boobs to my boyfriend. Oh wait, he doesn't own a magnifying glass!"

Stacy tossed the flyer in my face and walked away laughing. Stacy and her friends were straight out of *Mean Girls*.

Oh my God! Heat rushed to my face. I ran to the bathroom and began to sob. He lied. Bobby lied to me. I went to my counselor and explained the whole story. She called my parents and Bobby's. I really just wanted it to go away, but she insisted that Bobby had bullied me and should not get away with it. Bobby was suspended for a week. I couldn't endure the thought of returning to Torrey. My parents agreed to let me start anew at La Costa High School, but even then my self-confidence had shattered. So I just focused on my school work and participated in some sports at my new school. The following three years I barely spoke to any boys, much less had a boyfriend. So I got through high school as best I could, and suddenly graduation was upon me.

CHAPTER TWO

I KNEW THAT I WANTED TO GO TO COLLEGE FAR AWAY. I had always loved going to visit my grandparents up in Oregon so I thought that would be a good place to apply.

I was thrilled when I was accepted to Oregon State University, in Corvallis, Oregon. Although I loved San Diego, I had to get away. I needed to heal my self-confidence. My first year at college was wonderful. I had decided to major in English. I wasn't really sure what I wanted to do after college, but I had always loved English.

I made friends quickly and joined some extracurricular sports. Flag football was my favorite. I was feeling more like myself every day. I met Brian at one of the flag football games. I had grown used to avoiding boys due to my embarrassing experience in high school so I was cautious to let Brian get too close. I took some time getting to know him. We started out as friends and slowly began seeing each other outside of the games. Brian was great for encouraging me. He slowly helped rebuild my confidence, even though I still kept him at an emotional distance.

We dated all of my freshman year. Brian was from Corvallis so we would hang out with his family often. Brian was really wonderful. I loved him but for some reason didn't see a future with him. He had planned to always stay in Corvallis. Although I liked the town, I longed for the sun again. I spent the summer between my freshman and sophomore year in San Diego. Brian visited me a few times, but he sensed that I was distancing myself. When I returned to school in the fall, I ended it with him. He was devastated. This time, I had broken someone's heart. I felt horrible but had to do it. I hoped we could remain friends even though I realized it was very cliché.

Winter break provided an opportunity for me to study in Italy for a month. On the airplane, I sat next to my best friend, Ginny. We first flew to NYC and on the second flight we still sat together and on the other side of me sat Matt, a junior. Matt was very precocious. We got to know each other on the eight-hour flight to Rome. He was so sweet, interesting, and quite the talker! I liked him immediately. Ginny had taken a couple of sleeping pills, so she was knocked out the whole time. In Italy, we were based in Rome. We took a few classes twice a week and then were free to travel around. We stayed in dorms, and Ginny and I bunked together, of course, and Matt was right next to us. Many nights we stayed up late drinking wine and meandering around the streets of Rome. Often times we found ourselves sitting on the Spanish Steps until two in the morning; it was wonderful, but the cynic in me wondered when Matt would show his true self. He seemed a little too good to be true. Against my better judgment, though, I fell for him. We spent the whole month touring as often as possible. My favorite part was Santa Margherita in Northern Italy. It is on the Ligurian

Sea and simply stunning. The hotels and shops circling the bay are sprinkled with vibrant colors.

I found myself sneaking into Matt's dorm every night for the rest of our stay in Rome. I confided in him how hesitant I was to trust a guy. He assured me that he wasn't that kind of guy and would prove it to me. I felt good with Matt but also a little suspicious. Every time a pretty girl walked by his eyes would follow her. I had a gut feeling that something was wrong but kept telling myself to not be so worried. My past would not determine my future.

Matt and I spent our last two years of college practically without leaving each other's side. We moved in together, too. We discussed marriage but couldn't really agree where to live. Matt was from Colorado and hoped to return. I was longing to move back to San Diego. I did flirt with the idea of moving to Colorado, though. It was quite sunny there most days of the year and provided all the things I enjoyed: hiking, rafting, snow skiing, and just about anything outdoors.

The spring before graduating, Matt and I decided to travel back to Italy. I thought for sure he would propose. I had agreed by then to try living in Colorado. I thought it was curious that he never wanted to go to Denver when we visited. In fact, I had never been to his parents' house. We always met them somewhere else, like Steam Boat Springs.

Matt and I had a great time abroad but there was no proposal. When we returned a few days later, I needed to print something for class one night. Matt's computer was already up and running so I thought I would hop on his instead of waiting for mine to start up. While Matt was taking a shower, I sat down in front of his computer, and the shock of my life was staring me in the face. His email was open. Only, it wasn't an email that I knew existed. He had multiple emails from some woman named Ashley. The subject lines ranged from "I miss you" to "Can't wait to see you." It was sickening. I thought I might throw up. I had read around ten emails when I heard the shower turn off.

"O. Can you get a towel for me?" he asked.

I couldn't face him. I had to flee. I grabbed my keys and burst out the front door. I left the computer open.

I received a text from Matt about five minutes later begging me to return; he claimed he could explain.

I didn't respond. I drove to Ginny's. The emails had dated back one year. What was happening? He had a double life? This Ashley person lived in Denver. No wonder we never went there together. Matt was planning to fly there the upcoming weekend. He had told me he was planning on fishing most of the weekend with his dad so I would be bored. I had bought it. I started thinking back to all of the times I "couldn't go with him" for one reason or another. Tears were pouring down my face by the time I reached Ginny's.

I didn't return home that night and didn't contact Matt. The next morning I went home early. Matt was asleep on the couch. I started crying again as soon as I saw him.

"How could you? I trusted you. We were going to get married."

With sleepy eyes, Matt begged on his knees in front of me. "Please, O. I'm sorry. I was planning to end it this weekend, which is why I didn't want you to go home with me."

"Matt, save it. You have lost all of my trust. This, whatever it was, is over. I'm going to get some things and stay with Ginny."

"O, no. Please don't do this."

"What? Don't do this? Are you kidding me? You've been cheating on me for how long? It's over, Matt. I could never trust you. Never. Let me go."

I pushed him away. He sat on the floor crying like a disappointed child. He disgusted me.

I packed a suitcase and grabbed some other things. I left him there on the floor. I couldn't believe it. I called my parents on the way to Ginny's. My mom said she could fly up, but I told her it was okay. I was going to see them in a month at graduation anyhow.

For the next month of school Matt tried to get me back. He sent flowers, would show up at Ginny's begging me, and wouldn't leave me alone. Finally, I guess he caught the drift. Of course I saw him at graduation. My dad and mom had to hold back from really screaming at him. I told them it wasn't worth it. My dad had to leave the day after graduation, but my mom stayed to help me pack up. I was moving home.

No one plans on moving back in with their parents—I hadn't, at least. I just graduated from Oregon State University with a Bachelors in Arts in English and wasn't sure what to do with my degree. All I knew was I needed to escape the clouds and return to the sunshine.

CHAPTER THREE

M Y MOM STAYED AFTER GRADUATION TO HELP ME
drive all of my stuff back home to San Diego. She
has always been my biggest cheerleader so was
thrilled to have me moving back home. My mom is quite
the entrepreneur. About five years ago, she started her own
designing company called Johnson Design. She'd always
wanted to be a home interior designer and finally made it
happen. Anyhow, her company was going gangbusters! She
is very successful and busy. So she and my dad sold the
house that I grew up in and moved to a nicer community.

Tommy, my little brother, was super excited for me to
move home. Growing up, he'd constantly bother me to play
with him so I knew there'd be a lot of jumping on the trampoline, swimming in the pool (no doubt a game of Marco
Polo), and playing catch with his Aerobie.

My dad is an ophthalmologist. He has a very successful
business; I don't foresee him ever retiring. Both of my parents instilled a strong work ethic in me. They were never
"given" anything while growing up and although my brother and I have never wanted for anything, we had to earn it,
too. So even though I was moving home, there were some

agreements: I can't live there forever and will need to begin to find work and figure out this adult thing.

Mom and I pulled into our driveway, and Tommy came flying out of the door.

"Sis! I'm so glad you're home. Will you jump on the trampoline with me?"

"Slow down Tommy," Mom said. "Give her some space. We just pulled in."

I laughed. "Tommy, I'm glad to be home, too. Let me take some things in and then I'll bounce. Okay?"

"Hi, Dad! I'm home!" I yelled as I walked in the front door.

"Hey, honey! I'm so glad you're here. Here, let me help you with your luggage."

We had an amazing dinner that night. I was starving, especially after the long bounce with Tommy. I could hardly keep my eyes open. I stumbled into bed around eleven and had the best sleep I've had in years.

CHAPTER FOUR

T**HE SUN PEEKED IN THROUGH THE BLINDS WAKING ME** up. I picked up my phone to see that it was ten! I can't remember the last time I slept so late. I rolled onto my side, sat up, and stretched. I stumbled into my bathroom to splash some cold water onto my face.

When I walked back into my room, I heard some commotion outside. I looked out my window, which had a view into the neighbor's yard. Mom said that some new people had moved in, and seemed to be very nice. They had dinner a few times, and Tommy got to know them because his baseballs and Aerobies always ended up on their lawn.

Just then there was a knock on my door.

"Olivia? Are you awake yet?"

"Yes, Mom. Come on in."

"Dad made pancakes. Do you want some coffee?"

"Yes. That sounds great."

I followed her downstairs.

"So, you've had dinner a few times with the new neighbors?"

Mom said, "Yes. Tommy kept losing his Aerobie in their backyard." She gave Tommy a displeased smile. "So, eventually we decided to get to know one another. Tommy has gotten to know one of their sons, Jack, pretty well."

After putting some clothes away, I went looking for Tommy.

"Tommy, where are you?"

"I'm outside!"

I walked out the French doors that led to the backyard. As I walked outside, a flying Aerobie came at me. I was quick to wrap it around my wrist. Tommy and I threw the Aerobie back and forth until Tommy accidentally threw it too high. It soared right over my head and landed in the neighbor's yard. Again.

We walked over and rang the doorbell. When the door opened, I could barely talk as the most gorgeous man was standing in front of me. He must have been 6'2" or more. He had thick black hair and stunning green eyes. He was also in amazing shape. I knew this because he answered the door only wearing his swimsuit.

"Hey, Tommy! Throw the Aerobie too high again?" He then looked at me and introduced himself.

"Hi, I'm Jon."

"Uh, hi."

"This is my sister, Olivia. She just moved back home."

I quickly added. "I just graduated from college." I didn't want him thinking I was some loser who had to move back in with my parents.

He smiled my way. "That's cool. I'm just finishing my last year at USD. Come on in. You know where to go, Tommy!"

I followed the two of them down a long hallway. We

walked past a room that had the door slightly cracked. I caught a quick glimpse of someone lying in bed. It looked like he was hooked up to some machine. I had stopped for a second but then the mysterious guy turned his head toward me. Embarrassed, I hurried and caught up to Tommy and Jon.

I apologized again. "Sorry about that."

Jon laughed. "See ya next time!"

As we walked back to our house, I questioned Tommy.

"Tommy, do you know who was in that room? It looked like he was hooked up to some machine or something."

"Yeah, that's Jon's brother, Jack. I have hung with him a few times. He has something wrong with him so he has to have oxygen all of the time. I think he has cancer or something. Anyhow, I'm going to play Minecraft."

"Okay," I said. Although I had only caught a glimpse of Jack, I did notice how attractive he was. I thought Jon was pretty cute, but Jack, even in that short viewing, was even better looking. At a glance, I could see that he shared the dark hair and bright eyes. I wasn't sure if they were blue or green. Of course, I had sworn off men for a while. After the disaster with my ex-boyfriend, Matt, I needed to be single for a bit. I still couldn't believe I wasted two years with him and all that time he was stringing along some other girl in his hometown.

CHAPTER FIVE

A WEEK HAD GONE BY SINCE MOVING HOME. I WAS finished putting all of my things away and had begun to think about my next step. I knew that I did not want to teach. A lot of English majors become lawyers, but that was out of the question, too. One thing I knew was that I was most happy when I was creating.

My mom's voice carried up the stairs.

"Olivia!"

I poked my head out of my door. "Yes, Mom. Up here."

"Honey, what are you doing today? I could use some help at the office and was wondering if you're available?"

"Yes, of course, Mom. Just let me finish getting dressed, and I will be down."

I was looking at my long black hair. I hadn't really realized how long it had become. It felt heavy. Time for a change. I popped my contacts in, pulled my hair back, and finished getting dressed.

When I arrived at the office, mom's employees were excited to see me. She had hired some quality people, including her sister, Aunt Lilly. Aunt Lilly was overjoyed to see me. She hugged me a little too tightly.

"Olivia, you are just so beautiful. I'm so glad you are back in town. Have you set aside some time to help us today?"

"Yeah. I'm not sure what Mom has in mind, but I'm here to help."

"Actually, I was hoping you would go with me to a client's house," my mom replied with a mischievous smile. "He is proving to be a little difficult, and I thought you could bring a fresh pair of eyes to the project. Your beautiful blue eyes," she said still smiling.

"Really, Mom? I don't have the talent that you do. I don't really know how helpful I can be. I'll try, though."

Mom clapped her hands together. "Fantastic! I need to grab the file, and we'll get going."

In the car I questioned my mom. "So where is the job?"

"Oh, it's in 4S Ranch."

"Oh, that's not intimidating at all." I jested with a small amount of sarcasm.

My mom laughed. "Olivia. It's fine. The man is very nice, actually—just difficult to please."

"It's just a man?" I inquired.

"Yep. He's pretty young too." She winked at me.

"Mom, you know I need a break after that horrible disaster of a relationship. I am not ready to date."

"Whatever you say, Olivia. Whatever you say."

Mom told me that he had inherited some money from a grandparent and then invested it into failing businesses. He turned the businesses around and sold them.

We pulled up to the gate. Correction, massive gate. My mom gave her name and the gate opened. The driveway was pretty long. It had the most beautiful cypress trees lining it on each side. It reminded me of Italy. It took me back to my trip with Matt. Too bad I had been with such a fraud eating and drinking my way through Tuscany. As we inched closer to the house, I couldn't believe my eyes. It was not only massive, but as if the owner had picked it up from the hills of Tuscany and placed it there in North County. I fell in love immediately.

"Mom, this place is amazing!" I gasped.

"I know. I have already completed his kitchen and living room. We are now moving to his bedroom." She winked again.

Giving her a wink back, I said, "Okay, Cupid. Calm down." Mom put her arm around me, and we walked to the front door.

We were greeted by Sumiko, a very sweet Asian lady. She knew my mom pretty well because Mom had been spending a lot of time there. Sumiko led us through the enormous entryway and out through the open accordion doors to the back patio. Again, my eyes were huge with amazement. I could not believe this place. I walked to the edge of the patio which looked down over a gorgeous pool. There must have been an acre of grass beyond the pool. Absolutely beautiful.

"How do you like the view?"

I turned quickly to see a man standing in front of me. The sun was shining directly into my eyes. I put my hand up to shade them and quickly picked my mouth up from the floor. There in front of me stood Jack, the man who I had glimpsed lying in bed when Tommy and I went next door to get his Aerobie.

"Um, uh it's incredible." I was surprised to see him. I knew that I was jumbling my words. And like I said before, he was gorgeous. The most beautiful man that I had ever seen. He was tall with dark hair, pretty blue eyes, and looked pretty fit even though he had an oxygen tank in tow.

My mom walked up to us. "Honey, this is Jack. His family lives next to us. Jack, this is my daughter, Olivia."

He reached out a hand. "Pleased to meet you, Olivia."

"Likewise," I said.

"Olivia recently graduated from college. She's moved back and is in between figuring out her career path. She's very creative and has a great eye so I thought I would bring her along. I hope that's okay."

Jack looked at me and smiled curiously. "Of course. Let's see what she can bring to the table."

We sat outside and Mom went over the most recent plans. Jack vetoed half of it. I could tell that my mom was getting frustrated so I decided to jump in.

"Jack, would it be okay if I saw the space? I could be of better help if I knew what we were discussing."

Jack agreed and the three of us stood up and made our way inside. We went back toward the entrance. Jack pointed at the two sets of stairs hugging the foyer.

"Pick your poison," he said and pointed to each side.

We chose the opposite side that he did. My mom was already near the top. I glanced over at him as he inched his way up the stairs. I could tell that it wasn't easy. I wondered what was wrong. I looked quickly away when he glanced my way.

"I'll get there," he said. "Follow your mom."

I felt foolish. I hope he didn't think I was staring.

As I walked around his spacious bedroom, I could feel the heat of his stare. Each time I looked his way, he didn't break his stare like I had. He was very confident in himself. He would smile using one side of his mouth as though he was curious about me, too.

When we finished looking around his bedroom, we walked back downstairs.

"Okay, Jack. I think we have some things to work on. Olivia and I will talk, and I will call you tomorrow with our suggestions."

"Sounds great, Liz. Olivia, a pleasure to meet you," he said as he extended his hand.

"It was great meeting you, too. Thanks for allowing my input. This should be fun." I flashed him a quick smile and walked away.

CHAPTER SIX

BACK IN THE CAR ON THE RIDE HOME, I QUESTIONED my mom about what had just transpired.

"Mom," I said. "Why didn't you tell me it was Jack?"

"I didn't know that you knew him."

"Well, uh, I don't. I did catch a glimpse of him, though, when I walked over there to help Tommy retrieve his Aerobie."

"Oh yes, he was staying there after one of his treatments; his mom is a nurse, so she insists he stay there."

"Treatments? What's wrong with him?"

"He has lung cancer. He already had chemo. It didn't seem to work too well, so they are trying some new treatment. I sure hope he beats it. He is such a nice man. Gorgeous too, right?" she smiled.

"How old is he?"

"I think he's 32. He graduated from Harvard. Like I said before, he's an intelligent business man. Dad has talked to him about it. You should ask Dad for the details."

"How did he get lung cancer? Start smoking at age four?"

My mom laughed. "No. I guess when Jack was 20 the doctors found a tumor in his back. It was cancerous so he underwent chemo. He went into remission for about ten years. Then, it showed up again in his lungs. Bad deck dealt to him, I guess. He is trying some different treatments this time. I hope it works. It would be such a shame to lose such a young, successful man."

I looked out my window and wondered why some people have such bad luck in life.

We pulled into our driveway just as Jon was leaving his. He rolled down his window. "Hey Olivia! How's it going?"

I waved back. "Great. Thanks."

He sped off, and I walked inside. I could not stop thinking about Jack. It made me sad that such a young person who had so much going for him was so sick. I wanted to get to know him better but had a feeling it might be harder than I had hoped.

That night I lay in bed thinking about Jack and also how I had sworn off men. Of course this had to happen. I don't even know why I was wasting time thinking about him. It didn't seem like his health was improving. Why even think about someone who probably won't live a lot longer? Then I felt bad for thinking that. Maybe this new treatment will work. Maybe a lung transplant. I felt my eyelids getting heavier. The next thing I knew, it was morning, and the sun was shining through the blinds once more.

Downstairs in the kitchen as I was pouring some coffee, my mom walked in.

"Good morning, sweetie. I just spoke to Jack. He has a treatment today so we won't be able to talk to him for a few days. He said that you could take your ideas to him while he is staying at his parents' house."

I choked on my coffee. "He wants me? What about you?"

"He said he'd like to work with you. It's fine with me. I have so many projects right now that I could use the help. He's easy on the eyes. I'm sure you won't mind," she smiled.

"Well, uh, I guess I could. When?"

"He'll call when he's ready. Probably a couple of days. The treatments wear him out."

I felt sick to my stomach. It was nerves I suppose. He wants to work with me? Oh, God. Maybe he just sees potential in me as a designer. Yes. I'm sure that's it.

"Olivia. Olivia," my mom implored.

I realized that I was leaning against the counter, coffee in hand, completely daydreaming.

"Yes, Mom. Sorry. Just thinking about the design. Ready?" We walked out to the car and drove to her office.

I worked on some other projects. Mom needed help choosing some paint colors and fabrics. I was really enjoying it. I started to think that maybe design is where I should be. I couldn't stop thinking about Jack, though. I was wondering if he was okay. Why did I care? I had only met the guy once, yet somehow felt a connection to him. Maybe I just felt sorry for him. Having cancer sure sucks.

That night before getting into bed, I got up and peered out the window. I was hoping to maybe catch a glimpse of Jack. The light was on in the room where he stays. I saw a shadow cross in front of the window. It came back and stood there. Then the curtain parted. There he was, peering out his window. I darted away from my window, scared he might see me. I got back in bed and sunk comfortably into my sheets.

The next day I was busy at the office creating some designs for Jack. At dinner that night, I told my mom that I thought I might want to work for her. She was ecstatic.

"Oh, Olivia! It is my dream to have you working with me and eventually take over the company. I'm so happy. I really think you have an eye for design. You'll be great."

"Thanks, Mom. I'm excited," I said.

My dad proposed a toast to us and we began to eat.

While we were eating, Tommy declared, "I think I will go visit Jack tomorrow. We need to continue *Harry Potter.*"

I nearly choked on my chicken. "You're reading *Harry Potter* with Jack?"

"Yeah, he likes me to read to him while he's recovering. I guess it soothes him. Then he and I talk about the book. It's pretty cool. He loves literature."

I cleared my throat. "Well, Tommy, that's great. That's pretty interesting."

CHAPTER SEVEN

I T WAS FINALLY THE WEEKEND. I AWOKE TO THE SOUND of the doorbell. I heard muffled voices and wondered who was there. I got up and headed downstairs. There in the doorway was Jon.

"Well, good morning sleepy head," he joked with a slight smile.

"Hi, Jon. What's going on?"

"Oh, I'm just here to see if Tommy is coming by. He reads to Jack sometimes."

My mom walked away from the door and darted upstairs to retrieve Tommy.

"Do you want to come in for some coffee, Jon? I'm sure there is a fresh pot brewing."

"Oh no. Thank you. I already had two cups. Anymore and I will be way too shaky. I need to study for finals. You're lucky you are finished already. We have one more week. Let Tommy know that he can come over when he's ready. See ya!" Jon said as he walked out the door.

"Bye," I replied. "Tell Jack that I hope he feels better soon."

Jon turned around, smiled, and gave me a nod.

Tommy returned home from Jack's around noon. I guess Jack had decided to go back to his house because I saw him pull out around twelve. I wondered when he would like to go over the plans that I had for his bedroom. I thought that I would give him another day or two and then call him. Just then my cell rang. I picked it up and low and behold, it was Jack.

"Hey, Olivia. I know that tomorrow is Sunday but I wondered if you could come over to work on my project?"

"I'm going to church with my family in the morning but could come by in the afternoon. Say around three o'clock?"

"Sure. That would be fine. I'm anxious to get this project finished. I appreciate it. See you then. I'll have some snacks for us, too."

When I hung up, my palms were all sweaty. My mom walked in and asked, "What's wrong? Why are you so flushed?" I felt the heat rise in my cheeks.

"Nothing is wrong. I'm going to get into the shower."

I skipped up the stairs, closed my door, and took a cold shower. What was this guy doing to me? I couldn't wait for the next day.

On my way to Jack's the next day, I stopped at Starbucks. When I walked inside, I saw Stacy Alexander. I quickly turned my eyes away from her. I hadn't seen her since high school. She always hated me, but I really never knew why. She looked the same but a little ragged and run down. She was two people in front of me. I tried to avoid any eye contact. I even left my sunglasses on. I saw her turn toward me.

"Olivia? Is that you?"

Crap. She saw me.

"Oh, hey, Stacy. How are you?" I said this with a frog in my throat.

"Well, I'm alright. A little tired," she said as a little boy tugged on her skirt. "Mommy, I'm hungry." She looked down and picked him up. He must have been about four years old. She looked sweetly at him.

"I know, sweetie. Good to see you, Olivia. I hope all is well with you." I smiled and they walked away.

Whew! I felt like I dodged a bullet. She always made me feel so nervous. She was a major player in the flyers that Bobby Pennwright had distributed that horrible day. Here she was with a little boy already. I grabbed my coffee and headed north.

I was thinking about how awful Stacy had been to me in high school. She was one of the "popular" girls. In fact, she was very much like Regina, one of the plastics in *Mean Girls*. She was always so rude to me. She even tripped me one time when I was walking down the hallway. I fell and all of my books spread out across the floor. I guess people can change.

I pulled up to Jack's house and rang the doorbell. Sumiko answered and ushered me to the back patio where Jack was sitting.

I walked slowly through the foyer into the back patio. He really was a gorgeous man. It was hard to believe that he was battling for his life. I wonder if he had lost that beautiful black hair during chemo.

"Hello," he said. "Come on over. Sumiko, please get Ms. Olivia whatever she would like to drink. Olivia?"

"Oh, just some ice water would be great. Thanks,

Sumiko," I replied.

He did that sly smile at me. My stomach flipped. I cleared my throat.

"*Ahem*, should we get started?"

He folded his hands in his lap and said, "Sure."

I opened my computer and showed him my mom's design and pointed out some changes that I had made. To my surprise, he made no vetoes. According to my mom, he was so difficult. We talked for a long time and before I knew it, it was nearing five. The sun was starting to slip behind the horizon. Two hours had passed, and I had hardly noticed.

"Would you like to change to a glass of wine? Maybe some appetizers?" Jack removed his glasses and his beautiful blue eyes were staring at mine.

"Oh, can I take a rain check? That sounds great, but I really need to get back. I am meeting a friend for a run."

"A run? Man, I miss those days. These lungs barely get me up the steps now."

"Oh, I'm sorry. That was insensitive," I said, feeling embarrassed.

"No, no. Please don't be sorry. It's just life. I'm glad you're able to go out and enjoy nature. No worries, please."

I looked down at my lap uncomfortably. "Uh, do you mind if I ask…"

He interrupted me. "No, go ahead. Will I live? Am I getting better? Is the treatment working?"

Again, heat rose to my cheeks. I really should not have gotten personal.

"The truth is," he sighed, "I don't know yet. I have one more treatment and then a test to see how my lungs look.

Hopefully, good news, right?"

I was so embarrassed. I told him to have a nice evening and that we would talk soon.

As soon as I sat in my car, I hit the steering wheel. Why did I go there? Why get personal? Ugh! Before driving off, I glanced up and there he was in the window, waving at me.

CHAPTER EIGHT

THE FOLLOWING MONDAY MORNING, I HEADED eagerly to the office. I was really enjoying the work. It actually didn't even seem like work; I was having such a great time. I loved working with my mom, too. We really were a great duo. Later that afternoon, I realized I'd been at the office all day and hadn't heard from Jack. By six I figured I should call it a day. Just as I was about to leave, though, in walked Stacy.

I'm sure I had a very surprised look on my face. She was carrying a vacuum cleaner and some other cleaning supplies. I know at this point I really had a confused look on my face.

"Hey, Olivia. Your mom didn't tell you that I clean the office for her?"

"Um, no. She didn't mention it."

"I ran into her about four months ago and she could see what a difficult time I was having. No one would hire me. We talked for a little bit. I told her that I felt badly that I had been so rude to you in high school. She smiled at me and asked, 'How are your cleaning skills?' Tears came to my eyes. I couldn't believe she was offering me a job. I was and am so grateful."

I could see that Stacy had really been struggling. I touched her arm. "I'm so glad we are able to help you. High school is in the past. Don't worry about it."

I put down my things, and Stacy and I talked for a bit. She told me that after she graduated, she met some guy from the East Coast at a party. They wound up having one night together and the result was her son. When she was six months pregnant, he decided that he wanted nothing to do with her or the child. He left town, and she never heard from him again. He claimed that he was an only child and both of his parents had died. When she tried to find him, she was unsuccessful. Her parents took her in and now help raise the boy. Stacy never finished college but has been working odd jobs and attending nursing school at night.

I told her again that I was glad my family could help her. It's funny how people hold high school grudges in their hearts when it's such a short period of time in our lives. High school is a revolving door. I suppose it's such a time of growth and self-discovery that we either forgive those who did us wrong or forever hold a grudge for the rudeness and possible humiliation. I chose the former.

A week had passed and still no call from Jack. I was trying so hard not to think about it that it seemed to be the only thing that I thought about. It was driving me crazy. I was thinking about going for a hike or something to try to clear my mind. I settled for yoga.

Sunday arrived, and I was excited to attend a Padres game with my dad. Baseball games on a Sunday afternoon with my dad held great memories for me. Walking through the stadium the smell of popcorn, hotdogs, and beer filled my senses. A great day ahead! Although the Padres do not have a great winning streak, the people of San Diego love to attend the games and continue to support their team.

As we arrived to the ballpark and made our way toward the beers, I heard someone calling my name. I turned but didn't see anyone I knew. I kept walking but then felt a tap on my shoulder. I turned around and was surprised to see Jack.

"I nearly ran out of breath trying to catch up to you!" he said, breathing heavily.

"Oh, I'm sorry. I didn't hear you. It's so crowded. Jack, do you know my dad, Peter?"

They shook hands but had met before.

I said, "I have been wondering when I would hear from you. You know, to do you, uh your bedroom." Oh my God. I just said "do you." He smiled, and I knew my cheeks were red. I tried to rescue myself.

"Are you feeling better? Want me to come over soon?"

"Yes. I'm well, except this annoying oxygen tube. I will call you tomorrow and let you know when to come over. Where are you sitting?"

My dad finally piped in. "We have some nose bleeders. It's okay, though."

Jack looked at both of us and said, "Please come with me. I have a suite. I would love to have you join me. There are only a few of us and plenty of room."

I stumbled on my words. "Uh, oh you don't have to..."

My dad interrupted. "That would be great! I've never been in one of the suites."

"Great!" exclaimed Jack. He and my dad were off before

I had any time to argue. A suite sounded cool, but I was looking forward to the day with just my dad.

Jack's suite was amazing. There were two servers and loads of food and drinks. I insisted he let us give him some money, but he would not have it.

I have to admit that it was a pretty amazing place. He was much more animated than I thought. Baseball really brought it out of him. We talked throughout the game, and he and my dad hit it off, too. When the game was over, we parted ways. He looked a little tired.

"Thank you so much, Jack. This was great."

"My pleasure, Olivia. I'll call you soon."

"Night."

"Night."

My dad didn't seem to pick up on anything. I guess he was too into the game and chatting sports with the other guys. If my mom had been there, she no doubt would have worn out her eye with that wink she likes to torture me with. When we got home, Dad spilled the beans before I even had a chance.

Mom looked at me. "*Reeaallly*?" she said with her raised eyebrows.

"I'm exhausted." I muttered, "Good night, Mom."

Again I found myself laying in bed thinking about Jack.

The next morning I arrived at Jack's. Sumiko opened the door and said Mr. Jack was waiting for me in his bedroom. I walked up the stairs and down the long hallway to his room. The double doors were slightly cracked.

"Jack," I whispered as I opened the door. "Jack, are you here?"

I saw a light on in the closet. As I approached, there he was. He was only wearing his boxers.

"Oh, gosh. I'm sorry. Sumiko said you were waiting for me."

He turned toward me. He wasn't hooked up to the oxygen. "She was right. I was waiting."

He walked toward me, took my face into his hands, pushed my hair away from my face, and leaned in. Before I knew it, we were immersed in a very passionate kiss. He pushed me up against the drawers. He slipped his hands under my shirt and slowly brought it up over my head. Next he slipped his thumbs into the waist of my skirt and slipped it off. He kissed my stomach as he bent down to slip my skirt off of my feet. He was pressed up against me still kissing me. He whispered into my ear. "Olivia…"

Suddenly, my eyes opened and I sat up to a loud knock on my door. I was breathing hard. It had been a dream. My mom was outside my door.

"Olivia?"

"Just a minute." I had to catch my breath. "I'll be right down."

CHAPTER NINE

I STUMBLED DOWN THE STAIRS. THE SMELL OF COFFEE filled my nose. My mom was packing up and getting ready to head out the door.

"Mom, I am so sorry. I guess I forgot to set my alarm. I'll go get ready."

"It's fine, honey. I'll see you when you get to the office. We definitely have some work to accomplish today. I have a new client; I want you to ride along."

"Okay." I took my coffee and headed up to the shower.

I could not get that dream out of my mind. Part of me wished it hadn't been a dream. How could I fall for a guy who was probably not long for this world, though? I really needed to try to stop thinking about him that way.

My mom met me at the office door. She was ready to go to the new client's house so I just followed her back out to the car.

"Where are we going, Mom?"

"This client lives in Del Mar. It's an older man. He lost his wife about two years ago and is ready to change some things in the house—specifically, the master bedroom."

"That's sad. Hopefully, we can give him a new man cave

then!" I said.

We pulled up to the amazing beach house. It was right across the street from the ocean. An older man answered the door.

"Hello, Bob. This is my daughter, Olivia. She is working with me now."

He reached for my hand, kissed the back of it, and said, "What a pleasure to meet you. You are just as beautiful as your mother."

I smiled, a little embarrassed. I had always thought my mother was a beautiful woman so this was a compliment.

We were about to leave when we heard, "Gramps. Where are you?"

Bob said, "Oh that's my grandson. Alex, we are in the kitchen. Come here and meet my friends and designers."

Alex turned the corner into the kitchen. I knew San Diego was filled with gorgeous men, but he still took my breath away. I thought, *great, another man to dream about.*

"Hi, I'm Alex," he reached out for my hand.

"Hi, I'm Olivia. This is my mom, Liz."

My mom held out her hand. "Hi, Alex. Liz Johnson."

Alex said, "Nice to meet both of you. Gramps is excited to create a man's space, right Gramps?"

Bob laughed. "Yes, Alex. If that's what we call it."

The two of them were cute. I could tell they were close. Bob revealed that Alex had moved in with him after his wife died. Alex seems to be a comfort to him. Alex co-owns a local brewery in Encinitas and is 28. Did I mention gorgeous?

As we walked out, Alex asked me if I like beer.

I looked back at him. "Yes. Usually IPAs."

"We have a great IPA at the brewery. You should come sometime. Here's my card. Give me a call when you plan on coming; I want to make sure that I'm there. I'll give you one on the house." He smiled at me.

"Thanks. That sounds like fun. I'll call soon."

Alex had his arm around his grandpa, and they both waved as we pulled away. I could feel my mom's eyes on me.

"That was nice of Alex to invite you to the brewery. You should go."

"Oh, I don't know, Mom. We'll see."

I probably should go. For some reason I felt guilty like I shouldn't go see another guy. I wasn't even dating Jack. I didn't know why I felt this way. I clearly would not have a future with Jack so maybe I should take Alex up on his offer.

The following week went by without a call from Jack. I did, however, receive a text from Alex. He asked me to go the brewery on Friday night. I texted that I would. I worked until six on Friday, and on my way home, my phone chimed. It was a text from Jack.

Olivia, I'm really sorry that I haven't been in touch. I had a rough week. I'm much better now though. Would you be up for coming over tonight? Maybe discuss design over a glass of wine?

Great, now what do I do? I really wanted to go to Jack's rather than the brewery. What should I do? Stick to my word? Make up an excuse to Alex? I could hear my parents in my ear: *Olivia, integrity and commitment are two of the most important traits to have. When you say that you will do something, follow through.* I couldn't help it though. I chose to shirk commitment, so I texted Alex and asked if we could meet up the following night instead. Then, I texted Jack and agreed to go to his house. I was so excited that I had butterflies.

My phone chimed again and it was Alex: *Hey, Olivia! No problem. I know Friday nights can be difficult. I hope to see you tomorrow. My shift starts at 7:00! I'll be looking for you. :-)*

As soon as I got home, I hopped into the shower. I couldn't decide what to wear. I must have changed four times. At seven thirty, I skipped down the stairs.

My mom asked, "Where are you going looking so pretty?"

"Thanks, Mom. Jack called and would like to go over some design."

My mom raised her right eyebrow. "Really? Friday night? That sounds like a good cover story!" She laughed.

Again, the heat rose to my cheeks. "Mom, he was sick all week and finally feeling better. It's no big deal. We are just having some wine and talking design."

"Wine too? I don't know Olivia; it sounds like a little more than talking about design."

I smiled and said, "Don't wait up!"

I was so nervous driving up to Jack's. Jack answered the door instead of Sumiko. He hugged me and told me he was happy I was able to make it. I followed him inside, and we walked out to the patio. There were beautiful lights hanging above and candles sprinkled around. The wine was waiting on the table amongst the appetizers. It looked so beautiful. It felt romantic even. I was talking to myself: *Keep it together, Olivia. Keep it together.*

Jack pulled out the chair for me. I looked up and smiled. "Thanks. This looks really beautiful. Have you made some decisions about your bedroom design? We could start soon."

He poured my wine. "Yes. I like your last design. When can the workers begin?"

"I will call on Monday. They should be able to begin sometime next week."

Jack said, "Great. Now that that's out of the way, let's enjoy the evening." He held up his glass. "Cheers."

We spent the evening talking nonstop. We really had so much in common. Conversation with Jack came so easily. Before I knew it, it was eleven. His yawn prompted me to look at my watch.

"Oh man, I should get going. I didn't realize how late it was. Thank you so much for the wonderful evening. I will call you on Monday morning and let you know about the plan."

Jack walked me to my car and opened the door for me. He gently grabbed my hand, and I looked up at him. He hugged me and whispered into my ear. "I'm so glad you came tonight."

His lips met mine as he pulled away from the hug. My heart raced. After a few minutes, he pulled away, and we looked into each other's eyes. I smiled. He tucked my hair behind my ear, grabbed my face and kissed me again.

I felt weak. When he pulled away, he said, "I'm glad you came, Olivia. I'll talk to you Monday. Maybe before that." He winked.

I said, "I hope so."

I got into my car, waved, and yelled out loud, *OH MY GAWD!!!!* I was on a natural high. I didn't want to leave. I smiled the whole way home. As soon as I pulled into the driveway, my phone chimed. It was Jack. He asked me to text him as soon as I was home safely.

Once I was home, I popped my head into my parents' room. My mom was still awake.

"I see you still can't sleep until I'm home."

She took off her glasses and looked up. "That's right. Have a good night?"

"Amazing. I'll tell you about it tomorrow. Good night."

"Night sweetie."

CHAPTER TEN

WOKE UP TO MY PHONE CHIMING. I REACHED OVER AND grabbed it. I had to grab my glasses, too. My eyes were still a little blurry. When they came into focus, I saw Jack's name.

Good Morning, Olivia. I really wasn't going to text you until at least Sunday, but I couldn't help it. I had such a nice time last night. Any chance you're free for a repeat tonight?

I was smiling as I read his text. I wanted to respond "YES, YES, YES!!!" I had already cancelled once on Alex and felt I shouldn't again. I could go to the brewery for an hour and then go to Jack's. Maybe I shouldn't be so available. I put the phone down and got up to take a shower. I waited an hour before responding.

Good morning, Jack! I wish I could come over but already have plans with a friend. What about tomorrow?

He responded immediately. *Of course. Do you want to go for a drive up the coast? I know this great spot for brunch. Come to my house at ten, and I'll drive.*

I was really excited and texted back: *Great! Have a wonderful day today, and I'll see you tomorrow.* ☺

He sent a heart emoji.

I put my phone down and was grinning ear to ear as my mom walked up. I looked at her as I took a sip of my coffee. She sat down across from me. She took a sip of her coffee but still kept her eyes on me. I couldn't help but smile.

"Soooo, how was last night?"

"Mom, it was amazing."

I told her all about the evening.

At the end of my verbal spewing, she sat back, smiled, and I knew a "Mom" comment was coming.

"Honey, I'm so glad that you enjoyed your evening. Jack sounds like a real gentleman. I have to say though, I'm concerned about you falling for someone who is...sick."

"I know, Mom. I have thought about that. I am so drawn to him though. I have been since the day I met him. What if he gets better? The treatment might work."

"I hope so. I really do. I just don't want you to get hurt. Are you still going to the brewery? Alex seems very nice."

"I'm going tonight. Jack wanted me to come again tonight, but I need to stick to my plans with Alex. I am going on a drive up the coast with Jack tomorrow, though." I smiled and took the last sip of my coffee. I jumped up and exclaimed, "I'm going for a run, Mom."

"Okay, honey. See you later."

I drove down to the beach for my run. I like people-watching at the same time; it makes the time go faster. I parked at Crown Point, did some stretching, and started out. I made the turn near the roller coaster and headed back. As I passed the Bahia Hotel, I thought I heard someone call my name. I stopped and turned around, and I was surprised to see Alex. He was running the other way, and I hadn't even seen him.

"Hey, Olivia. I thought that was you. I didn't know you ran, too."

"Hi, Alex. Yeah, it clears my head. I've been running for years."

"I was just about to turn around. Do you mind if I join you?"

What was I going to say? No?

"Sure. I am heading back to Crown Point."

"Oh cool. I parked there, too."

As we ran, Alex did most of the talking. He was really nice, but I couldn't stop thinking about Jack. We made it back to the cars.

Alex said, "I'm glad I ran into you. I'm looking forward to tonight. See you then!"

"Me, too. I'll see you around seven or eight."

I spent the rest of the day looking over the design of Jack's bedroom and creating some plans for Alex's grandpa. It was six before I knew it. I needed to shower still. I tried to talk my mom into going to the brewery with me. I felt like I needed a buffer. She refused. I called a couple of my friends, too, but no one was available.

Driving up the 101 to Alex's brewery made me think about Sunday. I couldn't wait to go to brunch with Jack.

I arrived to the brewery around seven. I really just hoped to have a beer and go. I figured that I would sit at the bar, but Alex had a table set up for us. Before I knew it, the waitress brought over some apps and six tasters of each kind of beer. I like beer okay, but not this much. I didn't want to be rude, so I tasted all of them but only finished four.

Alex rested his chin in his hands. "So, how is it working with your mom?"

I was kind of surprised by his question.

I responded, "It's great! My mom is so creative and great at what she does. It's been really fun. Also, I think I found my niche, too. I'm going to take some design classes at night so I can learn more."

"Oh, that's a good idea. Do you want to stay in San Diego?"

"Yes, definitely. I was so depressed in Oregon. It's so beautiful but the amount of rain and cloudy days are horrible. I'm so happy to be back to the sunshine."

He was just smiling at me. *What is going on here?* I wondered.

Finally, he said, "Well, I'm glad you're here. Cheers."

He raised his glass to mine.

We talked for a little bit more but the pauses in our conversation made me a little uncomfortable. Jack and I didn't have any pauses. Our conversation really flowed. I looked at my watch. It was only eight. What excuse could I come up with to get out? Thankfully, he was working.

"Well, I guess I should let you get to work. Thank you so much for the beer and apps. I really like the brewery. You've done a great job."

"Thanks, Olivia. I'm glad you came up. I hope we can do this again but maybe a different restaurant when I'm not working."

I swallowed hard. "Yeah. Sounds good."

We shared an awkward hug. Alex kissed me on the cheek.

I wanted to call Jack but held off. I got home around nine. My mom was surprised to see me so early. I sat down on the couch next to her. I told her I had a nice time but conversation was a bit strained. I'm not sure why. I told her I went from single to now two gorgeous men wanting to spend time with me. She patted my leg and said it didn't surprise her one bit.

Mom smiled at me. "I was about to watch a movie. Want to watch with me?"

I said, "Sure. Where's Dad?"

Mom said, "Oh, he and Tommy are at the batting cages."

I settled into the couch with my favorite blanket that my grandmother had made for me. Mom pressed "play."

CHAPTER ELEVEN

I WOKE UP EARLY ON SUNDAY. HONESTLY, I COULDN'T sleep; I was so excited to see Jack. I could hardly wait for ten. I decided to get up and go for a quick run. After getting dressed, I grabbed my ear buds, phone, and headed out the door. I decided to just run around our neighborhood. Since it was May, the usual "May Gray" still blanketed San Diego's coast. In June the clouds stick around most of the day; San Diegans call it June Gloom. The marine layer settles in overnight and usually burns off by midday, but often times it lingers like a bad cold. No one likes it. This morning I could see a few breaks in the clouds, so I was hopeful that the sun would come out for our drive up the coast.

I came upon a street that I had never been on before. It had a hill so I thought it would be a good challenge. I was almost finished with my run. Up ahead I saw a guy kissing a woman goodbye. A little boy waved to her and started for the car. As I ran closer, I could see that it was Alex. I darted behind a tree; I wanted to see what was going on. The two of them climbed into his car, backed out, and were driving in my direction. *Shit, what should I do?* As they came closer, I inched my way around the tree, hoping he wouldn't see me. He passed by. Whew! Is Alex married? Is that his little boy? What was that? I ran home quickly.

I was out of breath when I reached the house.

"Mom! Mom! Where are you?"

She yelled back. "In the backyard. Are you okay?"

I ran to the back.

"Mom, you're never going to believe this. I just saw Alex."

She broke in. "Oh, how nice. How is he?"

I held up my hand. "No, wait. I saw him kissing a woman and then this little boy got into his car with him."

Mom stopped pruning her flowers. "What? What's that all about?"

"Exactly," I agreed. "Weird, right?"

"Well, maybe it's a sister or a friend. Give him the benefit of the doubt. I know he isn't married; he lives with his grandfather."

"Well, it was weird."

Just then my phone chimed. It was Alex!

He texted that he was busy today but hoped to get together with me soon. He said he would be in touch.

Great. Now what? How should I respond? *No, you loser. Why didn't you tell me that you're married? Or, why don't you just go out with that woman that I just saw you kissing?* I couldn't respond. I didn't know what to say.

"Well, I'm going up to shower. I need to be at Jack's by ten."

"Okay, sweetie." She returned to her pruning.

CHAPTER TWELVE

I PULLED INTO JACK'S DRIVEWAY RIGHT ON TIME. He didn't even give me a chance to go inside.

"Good morning, beautiful." He leaned in and kissed me.

I smiled at him. "Good morning."

"This way please," he said as he led me to the garage. There in front of me was one of the most beautiful cars I have ever seen: a baby blue 1960 convertible Corvette. It took my breath away. It was in pristine shape.

"Wow, this is so gorgeous."

"Thanks. I bought it last year. Are you ready, my lady?" He opened my door and motioned for me to get in.

"Thank you, sir," I said.

The weather turned out to be perfect. The sun was shining down on us as we cruised up the 101. I couldn't help but grin from ear to ear.

Jack cut over across Interstate 5.

"I thought we were going somewhere in Encinitas?"

"Well, I wanted to drive up the coast, but now we are heading to one of my favorite hotels."

"Hotels? Don't you think that's a little presumptuous?" I

asked as I lowered my glasses so he could see my eyes.

Jack started laughing. "It's nothing like that. The hotel has an amazing brunch. We can do the hotel room on our third date." He winked. I couldn't help but smile.

We pulled up to the Omni La Costa Resort, the valet took the car, and then we walked into the colossal foyer of the hotel. I looked up to see a magnificent sparkling chandelier. Jack grabbed my hand and led me to the patio.

"Hello, Mr. Fall. Welcome back."

Jack said, "Hello. Thank you. It's good to be back."

We walked out to a very private table overlooking the pool. In the middle of the table were my favorite flowers: stargazer lilies. Jack had phoned my mom earlier to ask her what my favorite flower was.

Of course we had an amazing lunch. He held my hand as often as possible. As we finished, he leaned over and kissed my neck.

"I would like to walk around the beautiful grounds, but I don't think I have the energy."

I said, "That's okay. I have had a wonderful time. I don't need a walk."

"Is there anywhere else you would like to go, sweetie?" he said.

"Not that I can think of," I said.

"Well, should we head back? I'm kind of tired."

"Sure. Of course. Should I drive?"

He smiled at me. "I'm not that tired." We both laughed.

Although I was hoping to spend the rest of the day with Jack, I understood that he needed some rest. As soon as we returned to his house, we walked over toward my car. I told him that I was going to let him rest. He gently grabbed my face and kissed me, again making my knees weak.

He pulled away. "Sorry. I would like to spend more time with you today, but I need to rest. I hope you understand. Can I call you later?"

"Yes. Of course. Go get some sleep." I reached up and gave him one more kiss. "Talk to you soon."

I climbed into my car, waved, and drove away. In my rearview mirror I could see him walking slowly to the front door.

Before I reached the end of the driveway, I had a text from him: *Text me when you are home safely. What an amazing day!*

CHAPTER THIRTEEN

ONDAY MORNING CAME, AND I KNEW IT WOULD BE a busy day. I had to make sure the workers got started on Jack's project, and I had to drive up to Bob's house. I figured Alex would be there; I really didn't know what to say to him. I had never texted him back.

It was nine, and I still hadn't heard from Jack. He must be tired. I sent him a text to let him know that the contractor and I would be at his place at three. At ten, I headed up to Bob's house.

When I pulled up, Alex was outside watering some flowers. He smiled and waved. I'm usually a pretty straightforward person, but I was feeling nervous to approach the topic of Alex kissing that woman. I stepped out of the car.

"Hey, Olivia! How are you?"

"Alex. Fine. You?"

I knew I was being curt. I think he sensed it, too.

"I'm well, thanks. I never heard back from you. Been busy?"

"Yes, I had a really busy weekend. Is your grandpa home?"

"Yes. He's inside. I'll take you in."

I followed him into the house.

"Can I get you something to drink?"

I asked for a glass of water and sat down on the couch to wait for Bob.

A few minutes later, Bob walked in with the water.

"Here you go. How are you dear?" He sat down in the chair across from me.

I proceeded to show him the plans for the bedroom. He liked all of it.

After approving the plans, he said, "I really want Alex to work with you on this too. He has a great eye for design. I'm sure you noticed when you went to the brewery. Is that okay with you?"

What was I going to say? *No, your lying grandson cannot get near me!*

"Sure. That's fine," I said reluctantly.

I walked into the kitchen to put away my glass, and Alex was sitting at the table.

"Your grandfather said that you would like to help."

"I would. Is that okay with you?"

I put one hand on my hip. "It is, but I think we should clear the air first."

Alex had a puzzled look on his face. "What do you mean?"

"I saw you, Alex. I saw you kissing that woman. Who was that little boy? Are you married?"

He started laughing, which made me even angrier. I glared at him.

"Olivia, I am not married. I was. Yes, that's my ex-wife. I don't know you that well yet, so telling you about my divorce and the fact that I have a five-year-old wasn't really a conversation I was ready to have. We are friends. Good friends. Marriage just didn't work for us. I kissed her on her cheek. Nothing else."

I really felt stupid. My cheeks were on fire. I lowered my eyes to the floor.

"Alex, I'm so embarrassed. I'm sorry."

He laughed again, got up, and came over to me. He hugged me and said, "It's okay. It's sweet that you were so upset." He pulled away. I thought he was going to try to kiss me. *Oh no*, I thought. He smiled and I backed away.

"Well, now that I made a fool of myself. Let's go up to your grandpa's bedroom."

"Whoa, I don't usually move that quickly," he joked with a crooked smile.

I hit him on the shoulder and said, "To look at the design, Alex." He started laughing, and we walked upstairs.

Alex was actually pretty funny. We laughed a lot while discussing the design. He kept making jokes about it being his grandpa's new "love lair." He even thought we should put mirrors on the ceiling and order a heart-shaped bed. I was crying at one point from laughing so hard. This encounter was much better than at the brewery. I really enjoyed Alex's company and his sense of humor.

I was curious about his ex-wife. I asked, "Alex, may I ask why you and your ex divorced?"

He looked at me and sighed. "You know, I really loved her and still do. We had a good thing for awhile, but we were young. We realized soon after getting married that we probably shouldn't have. She was pregnant though, so we decided to try and make it work. She's a great mom but not a good wife. I wasn't a good husband either to be fair. So, we decided to go our separate ways. We share custody with Brody. It's 50/50. When I have him, I do my best to focus on him. I have never introduced him to a girl who I am dating. Not that I date a lot of people."

We were sitting on the edge of his grandfather's bed. I grabbed his hand and said, "Thanks for telling me. I think it's great that you two are so amicable when it could be bad."

There was an awkward moment between us. I thought he might lean in. I thought about Jack and stood up quickly.

"Well, I should get going."

We walked downstairs. It was about two by then, and I needed to get ready to go to Jack's house.

Alex grabbed my hand at the bottom of the stairs. I turned around to find him right in front of me. Before I knew it, he was kissing me. I didn't want to kiss back but for some reason I did.

He pulled away and asked, "So, are you going to go out with me again?" He still had one hand around my waist.

I looked up at him and cleared my throat.

"Um, I am not sure. I don't usually date clients," I lied.

"Technically, I'm not your client. I'm more like your boy slave for my grandpa's project." He raised his eyebrows.

"I don't know. We'll see." I turned around. "Right now, I need to get to another appointment."

He was still holding my hand and let it slip away slowly. I was looking back at him. I knew I was flirting but couldn't stop. His piercing blue eyes had drawn me in.

Alex followed me out to my car. Bob was out there

finishing the watering.

"Goodbye, Bob. I think we got some good work done. I should be able to start next week. It would be a good idea for you to start packing up your room. We need a blank slate."

"Great, Olivia. Thanks for your help. I hope Alex was a help too. If not, just kick him out!"

"Very funny, Gramps," Alex said.

Alex opened my car door for me. "I'll call you later," he said.

I climbed into the driver's seat. "Okay. Bye."

I shut the door and waved goodbye.

Oh no. Oh my gosh. Why is this happening? I really didn't want to go out with Alex, but that kiss was pretty intoxicating. Then there's Jack. I have never felt this connection to someone before. I couldn't help but think about his current health though. Am I a fool to start something with him?

It was almost three so I drove up to Jack's.

CHAPTER FOURTEEN

I RANG THE DOORBELL, AND SUMIKO ANSWERED. SHE told me Jack was on the back patio so I walked out through the open doors and saw him sitting in the sun. I startled him as I touched his shoulder.

"Oh, sorry to scare you. How are you?"

"Olivia." He got up, hugged me, and then gave me another amazing kiss.

"I didn't realize you were here. I guess I dozed off for a bit. Sit down."

"Are you feeling okay?" I was feeling worried.

"Yes, actually. I feel good. I didn't sleep that well last night, so the warmth on my face caused me to close my eyes."

"Good. The contractor should be here soon, and we can get started."

Just then Sumiko walked out with Gerald, the contractor. I stood up.

"Hi, Gerald. Jack, this is Gerald. Gerald, Jack."

They shook hands. I've known Gerald since I was a teenager. He has done a lot of work for my family and now worked for my mom's business.

It was about five before we were finished going over the plan. Gerald left and Jack asked me to stay for dinner. Of course I agreed.

Jack met Sumiko in the kitchen and told her, "Sumiko, you can go. Thank you for your help today."

She said, "Mr. Jack, you don't want me to make dinner?"

He patted her on the shoulder. "No thanks. Olivia and I are going to cook." He smiled at me.

Sumiko grabbed her things, said goodbye, and left.

I looked curiously at Jack, "So *we* are cooking?"

"Yes, I love cooking. You?"

"Actually, it's one of my favorite things to do— with a glass of wine of course." I smiled.

He grabbed my hand and led me over to a door near the pantry. He opened it and a staircase wound down to an amazing wine cellar. Each step down revealed the enormity of the cellar. I could not believe how big and beautiful it was.

Jack swept his hand over all of the shelves. "Pick your poison!" He pointed in the direction of the vast collection of red wines. He knew that I didn't care for white so he didn't bother with them. I chose a Cabernet. He grabbed two bottles and motioned for me to go back up. "Shall we?"

He had bought two steaks, and I made some potato gratin and a salad while he grilled. We had one bottle gone before sitting down to eat. Luckily we had some apps while we cooked, otherwise I would have been dizzy from the wine. I wondered if he should be drinking. He told me that he could have a little and pointed out that he had only had one glass of the bottle. I was embarrassed that I guzzled so much.

We sat outside under the hanging lights and surrounding candles. Dinner was as delicious as was the company.

"I'm going to have to slow down on this wine, or I won't be able to drive home."

Jack smiled at me. "You can stay the night."

I smiled back. "Uh, I'm not sure about that."

"What? I have plenty of guest rooms."

I had assumed he meant with him. There I was embarrassed again. He just smiled knowing that he was the cause of the redness filling my cheeks. I blamed the wine.

"Really, feel free to crash in one of the rooms, if you want."

"Thanks. We'll see. I do have to work tomorrow, so I should slow down to avoid a headache anyway."

He sipped his wine, all the while looking at me. He put down his glass and said, "I'm hosting a fundraiser here in a couple weeks. Would you like to be my date?"

"That sounds enticing. What is the fundraiser?"

"The San Diego Zoo. I loved going there as a kid so now I help raise money for them."

"How great. I love the zoo, too. When is it?"

"It's June 12th. It's black tie."

"Sounds like fun. I'm in."

We talked for another hour. It was nearly eleven. I could see he was tired and so was I. I had stopped drinking and was just gulping water now. I was fine to drive so I said I should go.

He walked me to my car. As he opened my door for me, he said, "I have a treatment tomorrow. The doctor also wants me to try going off of the oxygen. I will probably be down for a couple of days. I will be at my dad's, if you want to come by. I'm sure Tommy will make his way over."

I said, "Yes, of course. I'll come and see you. Let me know if I can do anything. That would be great to be rid of the oxygen."

He kissed me for a long time, which made me want to stay.

I climbed into the car and drove away.

I had left my phone in the car and had two missed calls from Alex. He left me one voicemail: *Olivia, this is Alex. It was great seeing you today. That kiss wasn't half bad either, right? Call me back. I'd like to take you out this week. Bye.*

I should really tell Alex about Jack. But what were Jack and I? Also, I wasn't sure how I felt about the kid thing. I'm not ready to be a mom, let alone a stepmom. It was too late to call him back, so I decided I would call him in the morning. I texted Jack as soon as I was home safely. He sent a heart emoji back.

CHAPTER FIFTEEN

T HE NEXT DAY WAS LONG. I DIDN'T WANT TO GO TO Bob's, so my mom said she would go instead. I really didn't know what to do about Alex. I did like him but was falling for Jack. I couldn't wait to hear from Jack to see if he was able to stop the oxygen. I felt like I was keeping Alex at bay until I knew what Jack's health was going to be.

Later that afternoon, I texted Jack asking how the treatment had been, and if he was feeling up to having a visitor. He said Tommy was going to his house at seven and that I should tag along. I told him I definitely would.

I got home around five and I hopped in the shower. Then I went down stairs and had some dinner. Tommy said, "I'm going over to hang out with Jack later."

Mom said, "Oh great. Did he have another treatment today?"

Tommy and I both said at the same time, "Yes." Tommy looked bewildered and asked, "How did you know that?" he asked.

"Well, I have been spending time with Jack. You know, helping with his design."

Mom stabbed a potato with her fork. "It must have

been a good session last night. You came home around midnight?"

My face flushed again. "Something like that," I said.

At seven, Tommy and I walked next door. Jon answered the door.

"Hey, stranger! How are ya?"

We walked back to Jack's room. Jon pushed open the door.

"Jack, you have company." He barely opened his eyes.

"Hey guys," he said with a groggy voice.

Tommy sat near Jack. They talked for a little bit. I could tell that Jack wasn't really up to having us there.

I tapped Tommy on the shoulder. "I think we should get going."

Jack opened one eye. "Sorry. I'm just very tired."

"It's no problem." I said.

We started to leave and Jack said, "Tommy, will you leave your sister and me for a minute? Thanks, buddy."

Tommy said, "I'll see you at home."

I walked back over and sat next to Jack and grabbed his hand.

He smiled and squeezed my hand. "I just wanted a minute alone with you," he said.

I leaned over and gave him a kiss. "I'm going to leave you to sleep. Call me tomorrow."

On the way back to my house, I noticed Tommy sitting on the front steps.

"Hey, buddy," I said sitting down next to him.

"So, is Jack your boyfriend now?" His tone was interrogating.

I said, "Well, I don't know that he's my boyfriend, but we have been getting to know each other."

"You know he's dying," Tommy said with scorn. "Why would you lead him on when you know he's dying?" He was angry now and had tears in his eyes.

"Tommy, we don't know if that's true. The treatments seem to be working. Just because he and I are hanging out, doesn't mean he can't be your friend, too."

Tommy wiped away a tear. "Why did you have to go over there with me tonight? That's my thing."

"Okay. I don't have to go with you. I don't want to make you feel badly. You okay?"

Tommy looked up at me with his eyes welling up again. "I don't want Jack to die."

Tommy buried his head into my arm and sobbed. I felt my eyes filling up, too. I definitely didn't want him to die.

CHAPTER SIXTEEN

A COUPLE OF DAYS PASSED, AND I HADN'T HEARD FROM Jack. I knew he was recovering so I wasn't worried. I was hoping that the next time I saw him he would not be hooked up to oxygen.

I had just sat down at my desk when my phone chimed. I looked down hoping to see a text from Jack, but it was Alex.

Hey, Olivia. I swear I'm not stalking you. Gramps said you would be coming up today. Would you like to grab some coffee afterward?

I texted him back: *Hey, Alex. That sounds good. I'll be there around one. We can go after we get some work done.*

Great. See you soon.

I made it up to Bob's around one. I rang the doorbell and Alex answered. "Hey, there," he said. "Come on in."

He leaned in and hugged me. No kiss. Whew. Bob wasn't there. Just Alex. I thought, *great.*

We walked upstairs to Bob's bedroom. The workers had accomplished a lot.

"This is looking great. It looks like we are right on track," I said.

"Yeah, it's looking great. Now we just need that heart-shaped bed to arrive and insert the dancing pole!"

We both laughed. I walked into the closet to check out the work. All of the shelves were in and new carpet had been installed.

"This is looking…" As I turned around, there was Alex. He was making a habit of this coming up behind me business.

I jumped. "Oh, I didn't know you were right behind me."

He smiled and leaned in. He cupped my face in his hands, and his lips met mine. He carefully walked me backwards against the closet wall. He had his arms wrapped around me and pulled me in closer while kissing me. My heart was saying "stop this now!" My body was NOT saying that, though. I kissed him back. After a few minutes of making out, I pulled away. I wasn't sure where this was headed but knew it couldn't go any further. It was harder than I thought to stop.

I finally said, "Maybe we should go get that coffee."

Alex tucked my hair behind my ear and said, "Okay. Let's go."

"I just need to go to the bathroom," I said.

I looked at myself in the mirror. What am I doing? Why do I keep allowing Alex to kiss me? I need to stop this. My phone chimed. It was Jack asking what I was doing and wanted to know if I could come over later.

I sighed and walked out to meet Alex waiting for me in the entryway.

"Ready?" he said.

"Yep," I replied.

Alex insisted on driving since the coffee shop was just a few miles away. We stood in line and Alex said, "I'll order your coffee. What would you like?"

"I'll just take a small black coffee. Thanks."

I sat down on a comfy chair in the corner, took out my phone, and started to text Jack.

Hi! I'm so glad you're feeling better. I'm not sure tonight works. I need to catch up on some work. Rain check?

Immediately he texted back with a sad face emoji. *No, that's not acceptable. JK, I understand. How about this Friday?* It was Wednesday.

I responded. *Sounds great. I'll call you tomorrow.*

Alex handed me my coffee and sat down in the chair next to me. I asked him to tell me the story of opening the brewery.

"Well", he said, "I love to drink beer!"

I laughed and said, "No, really?"

He started laughing, too. "When I broke up with Amanda, my ex, I moved in with my grandpa. I was working as a manager of a restaurant. You might know it, Oggi's. Anyhow, I was mainly the bar manager. An opportunity came open for me to invest in the new brewery. So I took the plunge. I haven't looked back."

I sipped my coffee. "That's great! It's a really nice place. I know what you mean about doing something you may not have foreseen. I never thought I would be designing with my mom, but I absolutely love it."

I liked Alex. He was handsome, funny, successful, and seemingly a great dad.

The door to the coffee shop opened. Oh no, no. It was Jon. He spotted me immediately and walked over. I felt my palms get sweaty. I was about to introduce him to Alex, but Alex stood up and shook his hand.

"Hey, Jon! Man, it's been awhile. How are you?" What? They know each other?

Jon said, "I'm great. You?"

They talked for a minute and then Alex said, "Oh, how rude. Jon this is Olivia."

I stood up. "We know each other."

I leaned in for a hug. "Jon lives next to us. How do you two guys know each other?"

Alex said, "I went to high school with Jon and Jack, his brother."

No, this wasn't happening. No, no, no.

Jon looked at me. "Olivia knows Jack, right Olivia?"

And there it was. Crap. I didn't get to introduce Alex as my friend so now, of course, Jon thought we were on a date. Well, I guess we actually were.

I nodded my head up and down and said, "Yep, I do."

Jon said, "Well, look, I'm kind of in a hurry. Alex, great to see you. Olivia, see you soon?"

I said, "Yes. Definitely." I knew my cheeks were red. How will I explain this? Should I tell Jack? Will Jon tell Jack? Ugh.

After I left Alex, I headed to Coronado. Coronado was my happy place. I changed into my workout clothes. I desperately needed to go for a run. My head was cobwebs, and I was really worried that Jon was telling Jack all about Alex and me. I parked at the Ferry Landing and started out in the direction of the Coronado Bridge. It was a beautiful evening and perfect for a run. I just kept running and eventually found myself at the Hotel Del. I ran down to the beach just in time for the sunset. I sat down on the soft sand and watched the bright globe slip down below the horizon. I really didn't know what to do about this sudden love triangle I found myself in. Maybe I should say goodbye to both of them or write a pros/cons list. I ran back to my car. When I arrived home, I made a protein shake and went up to take a shower. The water massaged my back, and I closed my eyes. Suddenly, I was thinking about that closet. I opened my eyes quickly, turned off the shower and dried off. I climbed into bed and grabbed a book, hoping to distract my mind.

My phone chimed. It was Alex.

Hey, beautiful. I had a great time today. Especially, the closet wink wink! What are you doing this weekend? Dinner?

Oh no, no. How do I respond? I told him my weekend was really packed but another time would be great. He asked me to go to an event with him on the 12th, but I told him I had plans; it was the fundraiser for the zoo. We agreed to plan something soon.

I didn't sleep well at all. I tossed and turned all night. I kept dreaming that it was Jack coming into the coffee shop and not Jon. I have got to get this figured out.

The week flew by. Jack and I had a few dinners together always ending in me leaving and not staying. Unfortunately, he couldn't be off of the oxygen yet. Maybe that's why he hadn't asked me to stay the night. Alex kept texting to inquire about another date. I kept responding that I was busy. I guess I had hoped that he would get the drift. Although I really liked Alex, I was drawn to Jack.

It was finally the day of Jack's fundraiser. I had bought a new beautiful black gown. I couldn't remember the last time I had dressed up like that. I had my hair and nails done, too. Maybe tonight, I would stay with Jack, hopefully.

Jack wanted me to come a little bit early. I arrived around six even though the party was to begin at seven. Jack had never said anything about Jon running into me so I figured he didn't know. I wasn't going to bring it up.

I walked into the house. "Jack, you look amazing!"

He was pulling his oxygen tank. "Oh yeah, this tank is super sexy."

I laughed. "It makes the outfit!"

"Well, you, Olivia, look stunning. I love your dress. Come and see the setup. I want to know what you think, Ms. Designer."

I walked into a fairyland of lights. There were huge globe lights hanging from the trees. Dozens of stringed lights wound their way like cobwebs throughout the top of the patio. Beautiful bouquets centered every table. It was absolutely gorgeous.

"Jack, I love it. It's magical."

Around seven people started to pour into the house. My parents came, too. They had always taken us to the zoo and loved supporting the cause. My parents were set to be at our table. I was with my parents talking to some of the guests. Jack came up behind me, "Olivia, I want you to meet someone." I turned around and almost choked on my stuffed mushroom. It was Alex.

CHAPTER SEVENTEEN

A LEX WAS STARING AT ME. MY MIND WAS RACING. IT'S best to be honest.

I muttered. "Hi. Good to see you, Alex." I hugged him.

Jack was surprised. "You two know each other?"

Obviously, Jon had not said anything.

I said, "Yes. Mom and I are designing a new bedroom for Alex's Grandpa."

Jack smiled. "Great! Aren't they awesome?"

Jack wrapped his arm around my waist. Alex glanced down at the gesture.

Alex said, "Yes. They are really great. Please excuse me while I go find my seat and get a drink."

Jack said, "Yes. Of course. Great to see you. Thanks for coming. Did you bring a date?"

Oh crap. No, no. This was not happening.

Alex said, "I had invited someone, but she was busy. Good to see you, Olivia."

He walked away, and I thought I might throw up.

Jack said, "Alex and I went to high school together. Great guy."

I could see Jon across the way watching the whole interaction. I told Jack that I was going to the bathroom and walked toward Jon.

"Can we talk?"

Jon followed me into the house.

"Thank you for not saying anything. There really is nothing to say anyway. Alex and I were just getting coffee."

Jon said, "Olivia, I like you. I really don't want my brother to get hurt. He has enough pain right now. If you are even considering Alex, you should tell Jack. He deserves to know."

I said quickly, "I'm not. I want to be with Jack. Please believe me."

He grabbed my hand. "I do. He really likes you, Olivia. I know it's unknown about his health, but we have hope. You give him hope."

Hearing this made me feel so guilty. I had to talk to Alex and explain. Now was not the time though. I walked out to join Jack and my parents because it was time for dinner.

I was trying not to let on about how uncomfortable I was. I had a good view of Alex. He was sitting at the same table with Jon. I really hoped I was not the topic of their conversation. When Alex glanced back at me, I looked down at my plate, then at Jack. The night progressed with a raffle and silent auction winners were announced. Alex avoided me all night. Near the end of the evening, Alex was walking toward our table. My stomach was in knots.

"Jack, thanks so much for the invite. Great to see you and this is a great night and cause."

Jack stood up, shook Alex's hand, and said, "Alex, great

to see you. Thanks for coming. I really appreciate it."

Alex looked at me. "Olivia. Good to see you."

I smiled and said, "Good to see you, too."

I looked at my parents. My dad was oblivious, but my mom could sense the tension.

The night carried on with dancing, but there was no way Jack could dance with me. My dad knew how much I loved to dance so he asked me to join him on the dance floor. We had a great time, and mom joined us, too. Before we knew it, it was nearly midnight, and the band was packing up. Mom and dad had left about an hour earlier. Jack looked tired as he walked towards me.

Jack said, "Are you staying?"

I said, "Do you want me to?"

He cocked his head to the side. "What do you think?"

I smiled and said, "I think you are tired."

He said, "I just asked you to sleep over. Is that so horrible?"

I hugged him and whispered into his ear. "Okay. I can sleep."

After everyone had finally left, Jack and I walked up to his room. On the bed was a very cozy pajama set.

I looked at him. "For me?"

He nodded. "I was hoping to have a sleepover."

I picked them up and walked into the bathroom to change.

When I walked out of the bathroom, Jack was already in bed. He patted the side of the bed next to him. I climbed in, slid over to him, and laid my head on his chest. He had his arm around me, and I was asleep before I knew it.

When I opened my eyes, I remembered where I was. I rolled over to hug Jack, but he wasn't there. I sat up and looked around his bedroom. I called out. "Jack?" Just then the door opened. He was carrying a tray with coffee and some pastries.

"Well, good morning, sleepy head," Jack said as he sat down on the bed next to me.

I rubbed my eyes. "Good morning. This looks yummy. Thank you. How long have you been awake?"

"I always wake up around six. It's just my internal alarm. It's about eight now."

I took a sip of my coffee. "Last night sure was nice. Did the fundraiser raise a lot of money for the zoo?"

"Yes. It was very profitable. I won the silent auction item that I had bid on, too."

I was chewing my croissant so covered my mouth when I said, "Oh, great! What was it?"

"Well, it is a weekend for two in Napa. I was hoping you would accompany me."

I smiled. "Well, I don't really like wine, but I guess I could manage."

Jack laughed. "That wasn't you guzzling the wine last night? You could have fooled me?" We both laughed.

"When is the weekend?"

Jack responded. "It's whenever we can go. How about next weekend?"

I said that sounded perfect. He leaned in and kissed my head.

"I'm getting into the shower. Care to join me?"

I raised my eyebrows. I threw the sheet off of me,

climbed out of bed, and said, "Only if you'll wash my back." I winked and walked into the bathroom looking back at Jack.

He smiled and followed.

He had the most amazing shower, of course. It was huge with two shower heads, a rain head, and some water that could shoot out of the walls. There were even benches to sit on. He turned on the water, pulled me close to him, and slipped off my pajama shirt. Then, he took off his shirt. I slipped out of my pants and climbed into the shower. He closed the door behind me. I'm not sure if it was the hot water or the steam from us that fogged up the bathroom. We had to be careful since he didn't have his oxygen. Halfway through, we had to get out and go to the bed. Jack needed his oxygen. It got in the way a bit, but we just laughed. Afterward, we both were lying there, and I looked over at him.

"Wow. That's a nice way to wake up."

He smiled. "Yes, it is."

He pulled the covers up, rolled on top of me for round two.

I took another shower alone this time. I stepped out into the bedroom to put on my dress (I didn't have any clothes with me as I had not anticipated that I would stay over). Jack was dressed and sitting in a chair next to the window.

Before I put on my dress though, Jack pointed at the bed and said, "I hoped you would stay over. I took the liberty of getting those for you."

He pointed to the bed. There was a black top and a gray cotton skirt.

Just my style. I smiled, "Wow, Jack. Thank you." I let my towel fall. He looked at me and grinned. I put on the clothes; they fit perfectly.

Jack stood up and took me into his arms. "Do you have plans today?"

I said, "Nope."

"Great. I will steal you away then."

"What do you have in mind?"

"Can you handle a surprise?"

I smiled again and nodded.

We climbed into his Range Rover. Just then my phone chimed. I looked down to see a text from my mom. She assumed I was with Jack but wanted to make certain. I texted her to let her know I was fine and spending the day with Jack.

We drove up the 15. I guessed we were heading to Temecula. As we passed the last exit for Temecula, I looked at Jack with curiosity.

He smiled. "I told you. It's a surprise."

About 15 more miles up the road we took an exit just south of Corona. We headed west up into the mountain. The sign said, Glen Ivy Day Spa. This man knew what I liked.

"Have you ever been here?"

"No. I have heard about it and always wanted to go."

"You're going to love it."

When we entered the spa, I was amazed and excited to see three pools, two or three Jacuzzis, and multiple places to lounge. There was a hot springs tub, too, but I hate that sulfur smell.

"Mr. Fall, welcome. Follow me."

The attendant led us past the mud bath and up some stairs. We had our own private cabana. The employee told Jack to let her know if there was anything else we needed. He gave her a tip and assured her that he would.

I was so distracted by the scenery that I realized I did not have a swimming suit.

"Jack, I don't have a suit."

He motioned to a bag that was sitting on the table. I walked over and opened the bag. I pulled out a cute basic black bikini. This guy seemed too unreal. I looked at him. "Is this a dream?"

"Get changed. I'll meet you down there."

He pointed to a lounge pool. It was only about a foot deep and people were lounging and floating around on mats.

When I finally found him among the sea of people, he had a mat for me and a margarita.

I said, "What about your oxygen?"

He told me that he could go without it for about thirty minutes. He said the treatment was working. I was elated to hear that and leapt off my mat and jumped on him. We fell off and into the water. People were staring, but we were laughing. I kissed him and climbed back onto my mat. We soaked in the sun for awhile. Jack had to go back up to the cabana, but I stayed in the water. I must have dozed off a bit. Suddenly, I heard my name. I shaded the sun with my hand and looked up. It was Jack standing over me.

"I hate to bother you, but you have a massage in ten minutes."

"Really?"

"Yes. Here's a towel." I stood up and he wrapped the towel around me.

After my 90 minute massage, I walked back up to the cabana. There he was, lounging in the sun with his oxygen.

He heard me coming, opened his eyes, and said, "How was it?"

I said, "Glorious. Thank you."

"Ready for the mud?"

I laughed. "Sure!"

I understood now why he had bought a black suit for me. That mud was everywhere. It really did feel great though. My skin was incredibly soft. Afterward, we parted ways to shower and get ready to go.

On the drive home, Jack told me that he had hoped to take me to dinner, but he was very tired. I told him that I was tired as well and not to worry about it.

I dozed off during the ride back. Before I knew it, we were back at his house.

"Olivia." He tapped me on the shoulder. I woke up.

"Oh, I'm sorry I fell asleep."

He said, "I guess you're tired too."

We shared a long kiss and then I headed home. It was Sunday after all, and I needed to get ready for work on Monday. I was going to Bob's Monday morning to see the progress. I was NOT looking forward to that. I tried to get my mom to go, but she couldn't.

I was so exhausted; I fell asleep around nine.

CHAPTER EIGHTEEN

MY NERVES WERE ON EDGE AS I DROVE UP TO BOB'S. I hoped Alex would not be there. I pulled into the driveway. Alex's car wasn't there. I felt relieved but also knew I would have to talk to him, but wasn't ready yet.

The workers were there and about half way finished. Bob was drinking some coffee and watching the workers.

"Hi, Bob."

He turned around. "Oh, hi Olivia. How are you this fine morning?"

"I'm very well. You?"

"I'm great. This project is coming along."

"I just wanted to see how it was going. It looks like they are ahead of schedule. Alex here?"

"No. He had a meeting this morning at the brewery. He said to tell you hi and that he hoped to see you soon."

I thought, *sure he did*. He couldn't wait to call me the liar this time.

I was getting ready to leave and Alex was pulling in. Damn, I didn't escape in time. I couldn't just get in my car. I had to say something.

Alex got out of his car. I waved as he walked towards me.

He hugged me and whispered into my ear. "Well, if it isn't the little liar."

I pulled away. "Alex, I never lied to you. I wasn't even sure what Jack and I were until recently. You kissed me."

He smiled. "I don't recall you pushing me away."

"I'm sorry. I didn't mean to hurt your feelings. I really didn't. I like you very much."

He crossed his arms. "Here comes the 'but.'"

"I met Jack before you. I have really fallen for him. I'm sorry. I hope we can remain friends."

Alex said, "I'll think about it." Then he walked away.

I called out to him, but he wouldn't stop or turn around. I got into my car and drove away. I really hoped Bob didn't know anything. It would not be professional.

When I got back to the office, there was a huge bouquet of stargazer lilies on my desk.

The card read: "Olivia, I miss you already. Dinner tonight? ~Jack"

My mom walked up just as I finished reading the card.

"Wow, who put that huge smile on your face? Should we go to lunch and you can fill me in?"

I nodded. "Sounds good, Mom."

I told my mom everything over a nice lunch at C Level; it's one of my favorite restaurants.

"Wow, honey. There is quite a lot you have been dealing with. They both seem like nice men. Be careful with your heart."

I assured her that I would. We enjoyed our lunch and went back to work.

I had seen Jack every night during the week. We were

set to fly to Napa on Friday night. We were actually staying in Calistoga, which was about half an hour from Napa proper. I couldn't wait. I love Napa and wine, of course.

Friday arrived, and we flew to San Francisco; a car picked us up at the airport and drove us to Calistoga.

We stopped in front of the Mount View Hotel and Spa in Calistoga. It was such a cute hotel. Very quaint. Our room was beautiful. The huge king bed was inviting us in. Jack took me into his arms and started kissing me. Just then there was a knock on the door.

"Mr. Fall. Your dinner is here."

The server pushed in a table. He unveiled our dinner: steak, salad, and some roasted brussel sprouts with a balsamic sauce. It was delicious. I hadn't realized how hungry I was. We finished dinner around nine. I was exhausted.

"Olivia." Jack called from the bathroom.

I walked into the bathroom. He was pointing at the enormous bathtub. "Bath?"

We filled it to brim and were surrounded by bubbles. I was at one end and Jack the other. We each had some wine. There was a convenient small table next to the bathtub for our glasses. He put his glass down and began massaging my feet. I laid my head back and closed my eyes. He moved his massaging hands up my legs and pulled me close to him. His kiss was intoxicating. We stepped out of the bath and made our way to the bed.

The next morning we ate breakfast in the hotel restaurant and climbed into the car to tour some wineries. By the third winery, I was a little dizzy, so we decided to eat some dinner. The food helped to soak up all of the wine in my belly.

During dinner I said, "What are the plans tomorrow?"

"Well the hotel has a great spa and pool. I thought you could get a service, and then we could lounge by the pool. Sound good?"

"Yes. That sounds perfect."

As promised, we woke up, had a late breakfast by the pool, and I had a facial at one. After the facial, I walked out to the pool, smiling to myself thinking about how wonderful the weekend was and what an amazing man I had found. I looked up to see Jack sitting on the lounge chair. He was bent over holding his chest. I picked up my pace.

"Jack, are you okay?" I sat down next to him. He didn't have his oxygen.

"Where is your oxygen?"

He could barely talk. "I—I left it in the room."

"Why? Why would you do that? Stay here. I'll be right back."

I ran up the stairs to our room. I grabbed his oxygen and hurried back to the pool. When I got back, Jack had passed out. As I dialed 911, I yelled, "Jack! Jack!"

The ambulance finally arrived after what seemed like hours. They loaded Jack, and I hopped in the back of the ambulance, too. Jack was breathing but unconscious. I had tears in my eyes. I asked the EMT if Jack was going to be okay. He told me that they were doing what they could.

The ride seemed like ages. Jack was coming around when we arrived and opened his eyes halfway.

"Jack, Jack. I'm right here. You're okay. We are at the

hospital now."

He could barely talk. "Wha—what happened?"

"You didn't have your oxygen. You passed out."

He closed his eyes and was out again. The machines began beeping. They were unloading him quickly, and I was escorted to a waiting room. I called my mom and through tears explained what had happened. She asked if she should come up. I said it wasn't necessary, but I needed her to get a hold of Jon. She agreed that she would. My phone rang five minutes later. It was Jon.

"Olivia. What happened? Are you okay? Is Jack okay?"

"I don't know. No one has come out to talk to me yet. They won't let me back since I am not family."

"I'm getting the next flight up. I'll let you know when I land."

He hung up. Again, tears filled my eyes.

An hour had passed and still no word. Finally, at the two hour mark, the doctor came in.

"Olivia Johnson?"

I jumped up. "Yes, that's me. How's Jack?"

He said, "Come with me." I followed him to another room.

He said, "Please, sit down."

I had seen this plenty of times in the movies. They always take you to another room to give bad news. I started to cry.

The doctor touched my hand and assured me that Jack was comfortable and stable. He was going to run some more tests and was able to speak to his doctor in San Diego so he had a better idea of what he was dealing with.

The doctor put down his head. He looked up. "Olivia. Jack stopped treatments two weeks ago. It wasn't making a difference."

I was in shock. He lied to me? Why?

I looked at the doctor. "Well, what is going on then?"

"I can't give you any more information. I'm sorry, but that information is for family only."

Although I understood, I was very upset. I told him that Jack's brother was on his way. I also asked if I could see Jack. He said that would be fine. I followed him to Jack's room where he was hooked up to machines and resting peacefully. I walked over and grabbed his hand. He opened his eyes and smiled.

"Hey, beautiful."

"You gave me quite the scare," I said.

"Gotta keep you on your toes!" He smiled.

"Jon is on his way."

Jack's smile went away. "No. I'll be out of here soon. He doesn't need to come up. Call him and tell him to stay in San Diego."

"Jack, you weren't even supposed to be traveling. Why didn't you tell me?"

He closed his eyes and opened them again. "I wanted to spend time with you. Feel normal. I can beat this, Olivia. I'll find some other treatment."

Jack started to cough and a machine started to beep. A nurse came in and asked me to step away. She inserted something into his IV; within seconds Jack was asleep. She told me he would sleep so I could go back to the waiting room.

I sat down in an uncomfortable chair and fell asleep with my head in my hand. I woke up to someone tapping on my shoulder.

"Olivia. Are you awake?"

I looked up to see Jon.

"How did you get here so fast?"

"A friend of mine has an airplane. He owed me a favor, so he flew my mom and me up here."

I rubbed my swollen eyes and stood up. I hugged Jon and his mom.

"Hi, Mrs. Fall. I don't know how Jack is doing. I fell asleep."

"It's okay. I've talked to the doctor. They want to keep Jack overnight. We can take him home in the morning. Let's go back to the hotel."

"Can I see Jack before we leave?"

His mom said, "He is sleeping. Let's let him rest."

Mrs. Fall refused to leave Jack, so she stayed at the hospital. I followed Jon out to the car, and we drove back to the Mount View Hotel.

Jon had his own room, and I went back to mine and Jack's. The room seemed so lonely. I walked into the bathroom and started a bath. I sat amidst the bubbles while tears streamed down my face.

The next morning I woke up to swollen eyes. I hadn't slept at all. Jon was knocking on my door. He asked if I could be ready in thirty minutes. I agreed to meet him in the lobby.

I could see that Jon's eyes were red too. Jack and Jon were very close; I knew this was really difficult for him.

CHAPTER NINETEEN

W E ARRIVED TO THE HOSPITAL AROUND NINE. THE doctor wasn't going to let me go back to the room but Jon insisted. I was happy for that.

When we got to Jack's room, he was sitting up and smiling.

He said, "Good morning, beautiful." He glanced at Jon. "Bro."

I walked over to him and hugged him. I couldn't let go.

He patted my back. "It's okay. I'm fine. It's going to be fine."

Mrs. Fall interceded. "Jack will need to rest when we return. I will take him back to our house. I think it's best if you don't have visitors, Jack."

My cheeks warmed and my stomach dropped. By "visitors" I knew she meant me. She was always nice to me, but I would get a weird vibe like she didn't really want me around her son even though I made him happy.

I didn't say anything. Jack rolled his eyes and gave me a wink. I knew then that he wanted me to visit.

We checked out Jack and flew back to San Diego. Instead of going to Jack's, we drove to his parents' house.

"I'll stay at my parents' tonight. I'll call you later. I'm a little tired."

"I understand. I am really worried though."

He held my face in his hands. "I'm sorry our weekend was ruined."

My eyes welled up. "It wasn't ruined. Up to your ordeal, it was an amazing weekend."

He wiped away my tears, kissed me, and walked into his parents' house. His mom was waiting in the doorway for him.

I walked next door to my house. I collapsed into my mom's arms as soon as I walked through the door.

The next morning was Tuesday. I needed to go into the office, but I decided to walk next door first and check on Jack. I rang the doorbell and to my surprise, Sumiko answered. Jack asked her to help out.

She led me back to his room. I could hear some talking and Jack laughing. When I opened the door, I saw Tommy. He looked up at me with an annoyed look. His eyes were saying *this is my time. Go away.*

Jack looked over, too, but his eyes were welcoming. He smiled. "Good morning, beautiful. Come on over."

"Hi, Tommy. I won't cut in on your time. I'm off to work and just wanted to check in on Jack."

Tommy seemed to let down his guard.

I said, as I grabbed Jack's hand, "How are you today? Better?"

He coughed a little. "I'm just tired. I'll be okay. I'm going to see my doctor today and will know later."

Tommy butt in. "He probably wouldn't be so sick if you

hadn't insisted on him taking you to Napa."

I glared at him. Jack responded before I could. "Tommy, it is not your sister's fault. I insisted on the trip. Be nice."

Tommy and I had always gotten along so this was new territory for me, and I didn't know how to respond. I decided to go.

I asked Jack to call me later. I had to get some work done. I leaned down and kissed him. Tommy looked away in disgust.

As I was walking out I said, "Bye, Tommy. I love you."

Tommy didn't respond. I gave one last smile and little wave to Jack. He blew me a kiss.

This issue with Tommy was really bothering me. I decided that I would talk to him when I got home. He needed to understand my relationship with Jack. I'm sure it was hard for him to understand since he is only eight. He was territorial with his friend.

I drove to the office. I had to send some emails and then head over to Bob's. I hadn't heard from Alex since our last encounter. I hoped we could be friends. I know that is not what a man wants to hear from a woman whom he has tried to seduce twice. I was willing to try though.

When I pulled up to Bob's house, Alex's car was there. I took a deep breath and opened my door. The door was open so I walked inside. I could hear voices from the kitchen. I peeked my head around the corner and saw Alex and Bob. Alex's little boy was also there sitting at the counter.

Bob saw me. "Oh, hi Olivia! Come on in."

I walked in slowly. Alex looked over at me and then at his son. I thought *this isn't awkward at all.*

Bob said, "This is my grandson, Brody."

I put out my hand. "Brody, I'm Olivia. Nice to meet you."

He shook my hand and asked who I was.

Bob laughed and said, "Olivia is the designer of my new bedroom."

"Oh," he blurted.

He hopped down and ran out of the kitchen.

I looked toward Alex. "Hi."

"Hey. Ready to work?"

"Oh, will you be helping today?" I asked surprised.

"If that's okay?"

I smiled and looked at Bob hoping he didn't sense the tension between us.

"Of course. I'm glad to have you."

He smirked. "Good. Let's get to work then."

I followed him out of the kitchen and up to the bedroom.

Alex started to talk business, but I stopped him. "Look, Alex. I really don't want this to be strained. I like you. I'm sorry if you felt I deceived you. I wasn't sure, to be honest, what to do. I liked both of you."

Alex didn't look up but kept viewing the plans.

"You don't need to explain. Let's not talk about it. I need to get to work, so I can spend time with Brody today before going to my actual job."

Now I was annoyed. No more nice guy.

I snapped back. "You don't have to help me. I'm quite capable on my own. Thanks."

He looked at me from the corner of his eye and then

back to the plans. He mumbled something under his breath. I couldn't make it out.

He continued. "I think we should change the built-in cabinets in the closet. I think Gramps needs more drawers."

Well, obviously, the other conversation was over.

We worked together for about an hour. Finally, he decided to leave.

Abruptly, Alex walked to the door and snapped. "I gotta go. See ya later."

I didn't even have a chance to say '*see ya, asshole*' like I wanted. What a jerk.

I wrapped up a few things and as I started to leave I heard Bob call my name from the living room.

"Olivia? Could you come in here for a minute?"

His tone concerned me. I felt a lecture coming on.

"Sure," I said. "What's up? Is everything okay with the design and construction?"

"Oh, yes, yes. All of that is great. Thank you. I know it may not be any of my business."

Yep, here it came. Alex had told him what a horrible person I am.

"But, I couldn't help but notice some tension between you and Alex. Did something happen between the two of you? I know he wanted to take you out. You had coffee once, right?"

This was not good. What was I going to say? I didn't want to divulge anything for fear of Alex getting even angrier with me.

I carefully selected my words. "Well, Bob, yes, Alex and I did have coffee. We had a very nice time. I like Alex a lot.

He is a very nice guy. The thing is though, well, I have a boyfriend. I think that hurt Alex's feelings. Actually, you probably know him. Alex went to high school with him. Jack Fall."

Bob smiled. "Oh, yes. Jack is a great guy. Good for you. I'm sure Alex will be fine. I hope you two will remain friends. I know Alex really likes you. You might have to give him some time to recover his bruised ego. Isn't Jack pretty sick? I heard he is fighting hard though."

I wanted to tell him what jerk his grandson was being, but I refrained.

I told him that Jack was pretty sick but we were hopeful. I stood up and told him that I would be back on Friday to check on the progress.

When I walked outside, Alex was playing catch with Brody in the front yard.

Brody yelled. "Bye, Olivia. You're really pretty!"

I smiled and said goodbye. I got a small wave from Alex.

CHAPTER TWENTY

I T WAS ALMOST FIVE, AND I HADN'T HEARD FROM JACK. My first priority though was Tommy. As soon as I pulled into the driveway, I went inside and walked up to Tommy's bedroom.

"Knock, knock," I whispered.

He looked up at me and then back down to his book that he was reading. I walked in and sat on his bed.

"Look. I know it's hard to understand. Just know that I'm not trying to take your friend away from you. Jack and I like each other. We're going to be spending time together. I hope you'll accept it. It's a good thing. He'll be around more."

Tommy looked up at me with tears in his eyes. "Olivia. Jack isn't going to live."

I felt like he had just punched me in the stomach.

"Tommy. Don't say that. He still has other treatments to try. I think he's going to be fine." I wiped away his tears.

He said, "I heard him talking to his dad. I had to go to the bathroom before I left his house this morning. When I was walking out, I heard him telling his dad that he was done with treatments. He doesn't want to try anymore."

I had never felt this way about anyone before, not even my boyfriend of two years in college. I had only been spending time with Jack for a couple of months now. I couldn't stand the thought of losing him. Now my eyes were tearing up.

"Tommy, we have to hold out for hope. I'll talk to him tonight."

Tommy became nervous. "You can't tell him what I said. He didn't know that I was listening. Please, Olivia."

"Okay, settle down. I won't say anything about you. I'll just tell him that he needs to be honest with me."

I hugged Tommy, and he continued to sob on my shoulder.

"I know just the remedy for our sorrows; let's jump!"

He wiped his eyes and said, "Last one to the trampoline is a rotten egg!"

I still had my work clothes on but tore off my shoes and raced him outside. He won, of course. We jumped for a while. I must have burned 500 calories.

Mom yelled from the deck. "Dinner!"

We climbed out of the trampoline and walked arm in arm into the house. I had him back.

After dinner, I texted Jack: *Up for a visitor?*

Seconds later he texted back: *Absolutely!*

I put on some shoes and walked next door. I went to ring the bell but the door opened instead. Jack was standing there. He pulled me into him and hugged me so tight. Then he gave me a long kiss.

When we came up for a breath, I said, "Well, hello to you! That's a nice welcome. How are you?"

He smiled. "I'm well. I got some much needed rest. I will go home tomorrow. Come in. Have a seat."

We walked into the living room and sat on the couch. He had his oxygen with him.

I questioned him. "Well, what did the doctor say? Please be honest with me. I can take it."

Jack grabbed my hand. "Well, there is one more treatment to try. I need to rest my body for a couple of weeks before starting it. It's similar to chemo: hard on the body."

I couldn't help it. My eyes filled with tears. "I'm sorry. I said I could take it. But the truth is that I'm scared. I've never felt like this, Jack. I love you."

We hadn't said the "L" word yet, but there it was. He took my face into his hands and kissed me.

"I love you too, Olivia. I love you too. There is something else."

I sat back and took a deep breath.

"What is it, Jack?"

He looked down, grabbed my hands, and sighed. "I have to go away for the new treatment. I have to go to France."

Tears entered my eyes immediately.

"Jack. Why? You're not supposed to travel."

He wiped away the tears that began to stream down my face.

"I have no other choice. It's my last chance."

He pulled me into him.

"I don't leave for a couple of weeks. I would take you with me, but it's best that you stay here. My mom is going with me."

I looked up at him. "I want to go, but you're right. I can't leave for an extended time right now. How long will you be there?"

Jack lowered his eyes. "That's the other bad part. I have to be gone for one month."

I placed my hands over my face.

"A month? I can't stand to be away from you for more than a day. How will I go a whole month?"

Again, he pulled me back into him, kissed my head and whispered. "It's the only way, Olivia. I understand that there may not be a future here for you. I keep mulling this over in my head. Maybe you should see other people. I have no guarantee, Olivia. I just feel this is very unfair to you."

I pulled away quickly. I wiped my face in shock. "What? What are you saying? Jack, are you trying to break up with me but make me do it? I want you. I will wait for you."

He was tearing up now. "Okay. I was hoping you would. I love you so much."

CHAPTER TWENTY-ONE

THE FOLLOWING TWO WEEKS JACK AND I SPENT AS much time together as possible, but I still felt a distancing from him. His mom was around a lot, too, and I sensed she hoped Jack would break it off with me before leaving for Paris. I was practically living at his house. We even had Tommy come over a few times. We wanted him to feel like he was included. We had become the three musketeers, which we started referring to ourselves as.

Alex was still ignoring me. I couldn't believe how long he was dragging this out. It wasn't like I was that involved with him. I hadn't even slept with him. I guess he thought I was quite the hypocrite since I had gotten upset with him about his ex-wife. Still, I hoped we could be friends eventually.

The day had arrived. Jack's treatment was on the horizon. Jack was due to fly to Paris. My stomach was in knots thinking about being away from him for a whole month. He told me that I could stay at his house, but I think I needed my family to help me through the time.

I was so nervous. He was trying to comfort me when I should have been comforting him. I drove Jack and his mom to the airport. Jack said he could just get a car service, but I insisted on taking them. We hugged for a long time next to the car. I just didn't want to say goodbye. The airport security broke it up with the annoying "You need to move your car." We shared one more kiss and hug before I watched Jack and his mom disappear behind the sliding doors.

I started crying as soon as I began to drive away. I had to pull myself together though because I was on my way to Bob's place to check on the progress. We were nearly finished.

When I pulled up to Bob's house, I didn't see Alex's car, which was a relief. I walked into the open door.

"Hello? Bob, you home?"

Alex popped his head around the corner. Surprised, I said, "Oh, I didn't know you were home. I didn't see your car."

"I let my gramps take it to the store since I was blocking his car. Come on in. The workers are upstairs."

I started to walk away but then turned around. "Alex, can we talk, please?"

He was chopping up some onions and turned to face me with watery eyes. "I don't really know what there is to talk about."

I smiled, "Well, you don't need to cry about it." We both laughed. He put down the knife and washed his hands.

He walked toward the living room, turned around to look at me, and said, "Well, are you coming?"

I followed him, and we sat on the couch.

Alex said, "Look. I'm sorry that I have been rude. I

really like you, so it's not easy seeing you but not getting to *see* you. It makes it even worse that you're with Jack. Don't get me wrong, Jack is great, which is why it's so hard."

I looked down at my lap and back up at Alex.

"Thank you for apologizing, and I'm sorry too. I really didn't mean to hurt you. I hope we can be friends. I know that sounds cliché, but I do."

He grabbed my hand. "We can. Let's be friends, okay?"

I grabbed his hand back and smiled with a nod.

"It looks like you have been chopping onions too, Olivia."

I laughed a little. I told him about dropping off Jack and how long he would be in Paris.

He grabbed my hand. "I'm sorry. I really hope it works for him. I'm here, if you need to talk."

Just then Bob walked in. He cleared his throat. "Ahem, hi guys. Am I interrupting?"

I pulled my hand away quickly and stood up. "No. Not at all, Bob. I was just going to check on the workers."

He looked at Alex and then at me.

"Okay. Let me know how close they are to finishing."

Alex stood up. "I'll go up with you."

Time had gone by quickly. I had actually lost track of it. I heard my phone chime. All of a sudden my heart quickened. What time was it? I had gotten so wrapped up at Bob's that I forgot to watch the time. I looked down at my phone; it was a text from Jack. Shit.

Hey, Olivia. Forget about your sick boyfriend? :-) Just kidding. We are boarding the plane. I will call when we arrive. Love you.

I smiled at the text but also felt so sad and lonely.

I told Alex that I needed to get going. He waved and went back to working on the project. He was helping build some of the shelves in the bathroom.

I was about to close the front door when I heard Alex behind me.

"Olivia?"

I turned around. I *thought please don't go in for a kiss. I can't take that right now.*

He said, "I just wanted to tell you that I'm glad we're back to being friends. I had fun working with you today."

Oh, thank God.

I smiled and said, "Me too, Alex. See ya soon."

That day was one of the longest days of my life. I did fall to sleep pretty quickly. My eyes hurt from so much crying. My mom wanted to talk to me, but I just couldn't.

The next morning, I woke up to a text from Jack:

Hey beautiful, we made it. Paris is so beautiful in the fall. I wish you were here. Call me when you wake up.

Immediately, I dialed Jack. It rang four times before he finally picked up.

"Hi."

He sounded groggy.

"Hi," I said. "Did I wake you? I'm sorry."

He said sleepily, "Oh, I just dozed off for a bit. It's about six here. Mom and I are going out soon for some dinner. I'm sure I won't feel much like eating after tomorrow's treatment. How are you?"

I choked up a little but managed to pull it together.

"I'm okay. I miss you so much already. I will try to stay

busy with work."

He said, "I know. I miss you, too. It's just a month. We can do this. Right?"

I sensed some distance in his voice but decided it was jetlag.

After we hung up, I went downstairs to get some coffee. My parents were sitting at the table reading the paper and also drinking some coffee.

"Good morning, Olivia."

"Hi. How are you guys?"

My mom said, "We are fine. How about you?"

I sat down and told them I just talked to Jack. I was so worried but knew I needed to suck it up and be strong for Jack.

My dad doesn't usually speak up, but he cleared his throat and continued to tell me how much they like Jack but have concerns for me and my feelings.

I felt myself getting angry with my dad. He never says anything and this is what he decides to say?

I took a deep breath.

"Dad, I love Jack. My heart already is hurting. Please just let me handle this."

He looked down at the paper.

"Okay. Just know that your mother and I are very worried about you. We love you."

"I know. I love you, too, and appreciate your concern. I just need your support right now."

My parents both agreed to be there for me.

I didn't hear from Jack for two days. I knew he was probably sick and the time difference didn't help. I finally texted his mom. She responded that he was very tired and sick. She said he would get in touch as soon as he felt better.

On the fourth day of being away from Jack and not hearing from him, I really began to worry. I couldn't help but think he was distancing himself. Did he have to go to Paris? Was this the easy way out? I was sitting at my desk trying to work, but these thoughts were consuming my mind. It was about noon when I jumped at the chime of my phone. It was finally Jack. *Hi, beautiful. I'm sorry that I haven't been in contact. This treatment is kicking my ass. I miss you. It's about nine at night here. I sleep most of the time. Are you available to talk or FaceTime?*

I texted quickly back to him: *HI!!!! I miss you sooooo much. Yes, yes I can FaceTime. Call me.*

The familiar FaceTime ring sang out on my phone. I accepted and there he was with The Eiffel Tower glowing in the background.

"Hi Jack! It's so good to see your face. Wow, what a view behind you. How are you feeling?"

He smiled. "You're a sight for sore eyes. Well, sore body."

He turned around to see the Tower. "Yes, we have a wonderful hotel. What have you been up to?"

I said, "Just work. Tell me how it's going. When will they know if it's working? When are you coming home?"

Jack looked down and paused. I sensed something was wrong.

"Olivia, you know that I love you."

Oh no. Please don't do this, I screamed in my head.

"Jack, what's going on?"

"Olivia, you need to move on. I'm very sick. It's not fair

to you to hang on and wait for some sick guy to come back and probably die. You need to forget about me."

I started crying. I was sitting at my desk, so I walked out to sit in my car all the while pleading with Jack to stop.

"Jack, you're just scared. Don't do this. We are meant to be together. Please."

He looked down and back up with tears in his eyes.

"Olivia, I love you too much to do this to you. Please understand. I'll let you know when I am back safely in the U.S., but I can't talk to you until then. Please understand. I have to get going."

"Jack, Jack, please don't do this. I love you. I want to wait for you. Please don't."

I was in full-blown ugly crying by then. I could not believe I was waking up from my fairy tale.

"Goodbye, Olivia."

He was gone. I was numb. I don't know how long I sat in my car. I cried so hard. I jumped at someone knocking on my window. It was my mom. I opened the door, stood up, and buried my head into her shoulder.

My mom drove me home since I could barely see straight. I walked in the door and went up to take a bath. I sat amongst the bubbles remembering our bath in Napa. I cried again although I could not believe I had any tears left to release. I kept checking my phone hoping that Jack would change his mind. I had sent him two texts pleading with him. I even texted his mom. She just said that I should let him be for now and that she was sorry. I really wanted to wake up from this nightmare. My mom gave me some sleeping pills, and I was out.

CHAPTER TWENTY-TWO

THE NEXT MORNING I FELT LIKE MY EYES WERE swollen shut. My mom came in with an ice pack.

"Here, Olivia. Put this on your eyes. It will help."

"Mom, I can't believe this is happening. We love each other. This is a mistake."

"I know, honey. I can't believe it either. Do you think he is in his right mind? He must have all kinds of toxins in his body right now trying to fight the cancer. Maybe he doesn't understand what he is saying."

I paused and considered her theory but then said, "I don't think his mom would have told me to let it be if it wasn't true. I think she would have been surprised. It doesn't seem like she is shocked at all. Maybe I will go talk to Jon."

Mom patted my arm. "That might be a good idea. I'm going to get some coffee and get ready for work. Take the day off."

I took a shower and headed next door once I was ready. I knocked on the door.

Jon answered. "Hey, Olivia! How are you?" He leaned in for a hug.

I immediately teared up. He hugged me tighter.

"What's wrong? Did something happen?"

I looked up at him.

"You mean you don't know that Jack broke up with me last night?"

"What? No. I didn't know that. Come in. Let's talk."

We walked inside and sat in the living room. I was still crying, so Jon got some Kleenex for me. I told him what had happened.

"I'm so sorry. Jack and I are close, but he never said anything about that. As far as I knew, he wasn't going to let you go. I will talk to him."

"Will you, please? I don't know what to do. I'm lost. I love him. I know he is sick and may not survive, but I want as much time with him as possible."

I got up to leave and Jon assured me that he would be talking to Jack. He said that he would call me later.

I got into the shower when I returned back home. I just stood there feeling so confused as the water flowed over my body. I thought Jack loved me just as much as I love him. I wonder if his mom has anything to do with this. She has always been friendly to me but a little guarded too. Jack had once told me that his mom was very protective of him. Jack is a 32-year-old man though.

I decided to go to work. I had a new client and didn't want to cancel. My new client was in downtown San Diego. It was a nice respite from North County. I love downtown. It is so alive with energy. The new client lived in a condo near the Petco ballpark. She was interested in a quote to redo the kitchen and bathrooms. I rang the bell to the building.

"Hello, who's there?" A woman's voice rang through the speaker.

"Uh, hi, it's Olivia Johnson. I'm here to give the quote for the remodel."

Just then the buzzer sounded, and I opened the door. She was on the second floor, thank goodness. I was really scared of heights.

I knocked on her door and immediately dogs started barking. The door opened and an older woman of about 60s stood in the doorway.

"Hello, Olivia." She reached out her hand to shake mine.

"Hi, Mrs. Heart. How are you?"

"I'm well. Please, come in."

She hushed the dogs and ushered me in. The dogs ran off as soon as she snapped her fingers at them. She showed me the spaces, and we discussed her wishes for the remodel. I took some measurements and said that I would get back to her tomorrow. She was a sweet lady.

I was gathering my things when Mrs. Heart touched my hand. "Olivia, dear, would you like to stay for some tea?"

I usually would say thank you and say another time, but something told me to stay. I put down my things.

"I would love to."

Mrs. Heart told me to sit in the living room and wait for her. A few minutes later she came in with a tray holding two cups, a tea pot, and some small sandwiches. She poured my tea and sat down on the couch next to me.

"You know, Olivia, the love of my life died two months

ago." She sipped her tea.

I said, "I'm so sorry. What happened?"

"He had a heart attack. It was so unexpected. I still can't believe he is gone. We met when we were 20. He was a marine stationed here in San Diego, and I was studying to be a nurse. My girlfriends talked me into going for drinks after class; I wasn't much of a drinker but thought I would join them and have a tonic or 7Up. We went to this small bar downtown. We were sitting at a table laughing and telling stories about our day. There was an empty chair next to me and suddenly, a man sat down. When I looked at him, my stomach did flips. He was so handsome with dark hair, deep dark brown eyes, and a smile to knock you out!" Mrs. Heart was grinning ear to ear.

I said, "What happened?"

"He said, 'A girl as pretty as you should not be sitting down when there is such great music playing. May I have the pleasure?' He stood up and held out his hand. It was like I was in a trance. I placed my hand in his, and he led me to the dance floor. We were married two months later and inseparable until his death."

Mrs. Heart and I had tears in our eyes.

I said, "What a great love story. I wish I could have met him."

I looked down at my tea and could only think of Jack. The tears began to flow.

Mrs. Heart touched my hand. "Olivia, tell me who you are crying about."

For the next hour I spilled my guts to her. I told her that Jack was the love of my life.

After I finished, she said, "Olivia, you cannot give up on Jack. As soon as he returns, you must see him. I know that when he sees you face to face, he will realize his foolishness."

I hoped she was right. I thanked her for the tea and gathered my things. I said goodbye and walked out.

CHAPTER TWENTY-THREE

B OB'S PROJECT WAS ALMOST OVER; I WAS GOING TO drive up there later in the day. I actually hoped Alex would be there this time. I was so glad we were friends again. Hopefully, he knew that was all we could be. It was nearly five o'clock before I headed up to Bob's house. As I was leaving, Stacy was coming in. I hadn't seen her in awhile.

"Hey, Stacy. You're early today."

She put her cleaning supplies down and said, "Yes. I asked your mom if I could come in a little early. I actually have a date tonight!" She was elated.

I said, "Oh, that's great. How did you meet him?"

She picked up some cleaning cloths and said, "I met him at a brewery the other night. I was there with some friends, and he came over to our table. I thought he was going to try picking up on one of us but then discovered he worked there. Come to find out, he actually is part owner. His name is Alex. He's really nice. My friends had to leave, but I stayed and talked to him. I felt a connection right away. So, he called yesterday and asked me out!"

I felt a lump rising in my throat. Alex? Stacy? Really? It

had to be her. I didn't know what to say. All I could seep out was, "G-great. I hope you have fun."

She said, "Thanks! It's pretty great, too, because he also has a child. It's difficult to find men who have kids and who aren't married. I'm not so scary to him now."

"That's really great. Well, I need to go. Have fun on your date."

I walked out to my car in shock of what I just heard. He already shared with her that he has a kid? He wouldn't even tell me that. I was feeling annoyed.

Now, I hoped Alex wouldn't be home.

To my dismay, Alex's car was parked in the driveway when I pulled up to Bob's house. I sighed and said to myself, "Great. Just great." I decided I wouldn't ask him anything personal. Keep it professional.

I walked up to the house.

"Hey, Olivia!" Alex said as I walked past the kitchen.

I wanted to keep walking, but I stopped.

"Hi. How are you?"

"I'm great!"

"Good. I'm just going to see how the progress is coming along."

Alex said, "Wait up. I'll go with you."

I rolled my eyes and sighed as I walked away.

Bob was up in his room.

I said, "Hey, Bob. It's looking good. Just putting on the last minute finishes, right?"

"Hi. Yes. I'm very happy with the result. Thank you. I am sad though that we won't see your pretty face around here anymore. I hope you'll still visit."

I hugged Bob. "Of course I will."

I walked back downstairs and picked up my purse. "Well, I'll see you guys later."

Alex said, "Wait. I'll walk you out. I want to tell you something."

Oh great. No, no, no. I didn't want to hear it. Do I tell him I already know? Do I tell him what a bitch Stacy was to me in high school? That would be pretty immature.

I opened my door and threw in my purse.

"What's up?"

Alex put his hand on my door.

"I just wanted to tell you that I'm going on a date to-night. I know we are just friends, but felt like I should tell you for some reason."

I cleared my throat. "Alex, you don't owe me anything. You can date whomever you please. You know that."

He said, "No. I know. Well, I am excited about it, and I guess I wanted to tell my friend, too."

I said, "I'm happy for you. I hope you have great time."

I sat down inside my car.

Alex said, "Don't you want to hear about her?"

I turned on the car, opened my window, closed the door, and said, "Not right now. I'm kind of in a hurry. Jack is supposed to call soon (I lied). Later?"

Alex backed away. "Of course. Later. Give Jack my best."

I smiled and drove away.

Two weeks had passed since Jack dropped me. I kept texting him anyway. I told him about Mrs. Heart and that he and I were meant to be together. He would nev-er respond. I couldn't believe how quickly he stopped our communication. I spoke to Jon, but he said that Jack wouldn't talk about it. Jack told him to butt out even. Jon said that Jack might be staying in Paris even longer. I didn't want to move on.

I stopped at Starbucks before going to the office. While I was standing in line, I looked over at the sound of a laugh that I could never forget: Stacy. Then I realized that it was Alex with her. I couldn't believe it. I wanted to pretend to not see them, but it was too late. Stacy had made eye contact with me. Shit.

Stacy waved. "Olivia! Over here."

Just then Alex turned around and his cheeks instantly were red.

I waved and walked over.

"Hi, Stacy, Alex."

Stacy looked at Alex. "You know Olivia?"

He asked, "You do too?"

Well, this was awkward. Thankfully, Stacy didn't know anything about my history with Alex. At least I didn't think she did.

Stacy said, "Olivia and I went to high school together. How do you two know each other?"

She was looking at both of us. We both started talking at the same time.

"Olivia/Alex."

Alex stopped and said, "Go ahead."

"I am just finishing redoing Alex's grandpa's bedroom. Alex has been a big help, too."

Stacy seemed to relax. "Oh, that's great."

Just then I heard my name. "Vanilla Latte for Olivia."

Whew, my escape.

"Well, good to see both of you. That's my drink. Have a good day."

Stacy said, "You should join us."

I turned back around. "Thank you, but I need to get to work."

Awkward, awkward, awkward! I cannot escape this guy.

I was spending a lot of time at Mrs. Heart's now. I did a little bit of designing but mostly talking over a cup of tea. My whole life I have always felt older than I am. I connect with older people much better than those my age. Although I was beginning to second guess the continued pursuing of Jack, Mrs. Heart encouraged me to keep trying. I worried that I would become a nuisance to Jack though, and he would really dislike me. She kept reminding me that he wasn't in his right mind. Who knew what kind of chemicals were running through his body trying to annihilate the cancer.

Four weeks had passed now since Jack left for Paris. I still felt emptiness inside. I saw Jon once in awhile when we both happened to walk out of our houses at the same time. I knew he felt awkward talking to me since all I wanted to know about was Jack. He did tell me that Jack would be in Paris for maybe another month. I didn't want to bother him though, so I avoided him as best as I could.

It was the first of October now. The weather was cooler and actually raining. I was about to head out the door for work when my phone chimed. I couldn't help but hope it was Jack. I looked down to see Alex's name. I hadn't heard from him since that encounter at Starbucks.

His text read: *Hey, Olivia! I hope you are well. There are a few issues at my gramp's house. Are you free to come up today?*

I responded: *Hey, Alex. Yes, I can come now, if that works.*

He chimed back: *Great. Thanks so much!*

When I pulled in, I only saw Alex's car. I knocked on the door. No one answered. I rang the doorbell. Still, nobody. I tried the door and discovered it was unlocked. So, I walked inside.

"Alex! Alex, are you here?"

Just then I heard footsteps coming quickly down the staircase.

"Hey! I'm sorry. I had my music too loud I guess."

He walked up to me and hugged me. He smelled amazing like always.

I felt nervous for some reason.

"Is your grandpa here? What's the problem?"

Alex said, "No. He had to go somewhere, but I told him that I would show you. Come on up."

I followed Alex up to his grandpa's bedroom. I had a view of his very toned body. He had on a tight t-shirt and swimming trunks. No shoes.

"Are you going swimming?" I inquired.

"Oh, no. I just got back from surfing. Amazing waves out there today. You should go with me sometime."

"Well, I might. I have always been a little scared of the ocean."

"Ah, nothing to be scared of. We'll go soon. Okay, so here's the problem."

He pointed to the cedar lining in the closet. It was loosening in many spots. I ran my hand over it. I assured him that I would send the carpenters right over to fix it.

Alex was standing in the doorway with his arms crossed.

He said, "Thanks. So how are things with Jack? Did I tell you that I broke it off with Stacy?"

I was surprised. "No. I haven't seen or talked to you since I ran into you two at Starbucks. Sorry to hear that. What happened?"

He grinned. "She was a bit of a stalker. Sometimes she was pretty rude too. All of sudden, she just started acting like a bitch. She insisted that our kids get together, but I wouldn't. Life is too short for that bullshit."

I wanted to expunge how awful Stacy was but decided to just let it go.

Alex changed the subject. "So, you and Jack are good?"

I turned my eyes toward the ground. "Well, we broke up too."

"What? You're kidding. Why?"

I shifted my weight feeling a little uncomfortable. I told him I didn't want to talk about it and was hoping he would change his mind on his return from Paris.

Alex approached me and wrapped his arms around my back. To be honest, I wasn't sure what he was going to do. He held me close and said he was sorry. When he pulled away, he paused very close to my face. I pulled back.

"Well, anything else? I need to get to the office."

He stepped aside and waved his hand as to lead me out of the closet.

"Nope. That's it. Thanks for coming up last minute. When do you want to surf?"

I said, "How about this weekend?"

He clapped his hands together. "Perfect! Does Saturday afternoon work for you?"

I said that it did. I waved to him as I pulled out of the driveway. I didn't want to think about Alex in a sexual way, but he smelled so good and that body. Ugh! Am I being foolish? Jack is gone and seemingly doesn't want me. Alex is available.

The week flew by. I was nearing the end of Mrs. Heart's project. I knew that I would continue to see her though as we had become very close. I told her that I was going surfing with Alex. Surprisingly, she encouraged me. Maybe she thought Jack was a lost cause, too.

Saturday arrived. I bought a spring suit for the cold water. I would have to use Alex's board though. It was kind of a gloomy day. It was sprinkling a little too. As I pulled into his driveway, he was just exiting the garage with his surf board.

I stepped out of my car and said, "I need to change and then will be ready to go."

Alex gave me a hug and said, "Go for it! I will be right here."

Alex was sitting on the lawn waiting for me. He smiled as I walked up.

"You look cute!"

We walked across the street and down to the water. It was a bit chilly, but Alex was already waist deep. Alex looked over at me tiptoeing my way into the water.

"Olivia, you're waterproof. You're either going to get

wet from the rain or the water. Let's go!"

He walked over to me, grabbed my hand, and in we went. My heart was racing; I was so nervous. He put the board on top of the water, picked me up, and placed me onto the board.

Alex gave me directions. "Okay. Lay on your stomach. I'm going to turn you to face the beach. When a good wave comes, I'm going to shove you off and listen for me to yell 'stand up!' Okay?"

I said okay, but really did not know what I was doing. All of a sudden he was pushing me forward and then I heard Alex.

"Stand up, Olivia! Stand up!"

I did my best to balance. I actually stood up for about five seconds and then fell down. When I came up, Alex was right there. He took me in his arms as I was spitting out salt water.

"Are you okay? That was great!"

I was holding on to his shoulders and laughing. I hadn't laughed in so long. Through the water in my eyes, I could see his face so close to mine.

"Yes, I'm fine. That was fun actually."

We paused for what seemed like a minute but probably had been seconds. I had my legs wrapped around his waist and arms still around his shoulders. The waves were knocking us around, but he held on tightly. Before I knew it, his lips met mine. I kissed back this time and didn't pull away. The waves kept pushing us closer to shore. The rain was really coming down, so we decided to head in.

As Alex grabbed his board, and I said, "I feel bad that

you didn't get to surf, Alex."

He said, "I go all of the time. Don't worry about it."

We walked across the street to his grandpa's house. Bob wasn't home. We went in, and I walked into the bathroom. I realized that I needed some help with my wet suit.

"Alex, can you help me?"

He appeared pretty quickly.

"What's up?"

He saw me struggling with my suit. He unzipped it for me. I turned to face him and our lips met once again. Our wet suits and bathing suits came off. He held my face in his hands and looked at me.

"Shower?"

I nodded.

The shower wasn't very big, so we stepped out and before I knew it, Alex picked me up and carried me to his bed. He laid me down on my back and kissed me as he lowered himself down on top of me. His amazing kisses were just a prelude to what an incredible lover he was.

Afterwards, he was rubbing my shoulder as I laid my head on his chest. I felt bad, but I was feeling so guilty. I couldn't stop thinking about Jack. What had I done? Should I have done it? It felt so good to be in a man's arms again.

After some time Alex said, "Are you okay? You're quiet."

I looked up at him. "I'm fine. Not what I expected."

He kissed me again and I fell into his arms once again. We fell asleep wrapped in each other's arms.

I awoke to a loud noise that seemed to come from the kitchen. Alex woke up, too.

I sat up, crawled out of bed, and grabbed my clothes. I

turned to see Alex staring at me. I smiled and walked into his bathroom to change.

When I came back out, Alex wasn't in the room. I grabbed my things and walked out toward the kitchen. I could hear Alex talking to someone. I turned the corner to see Bob. I was really embarrassed.

"Hi, Olivia. Sounds like you and Alex had an interesting time surfing."

I think I had guilty flashing on my forehead.

"Hi, Bob. Yes, Alex is trying to show me how to surf. I think I got up for about five seconds."

We all laughed.

I looked at Alex and thanked him for a fun afternoon. I told him that I needed to get going. I told Bob goodbye, and Alex walked me to my car. He opened my car door for me. He pulled me into him and kissed me again.

He hugged me and kissed my neck. "I had a great time, Olivia. Let's do it again soon."

As I drove away, I couldn't help but feel very guilty. I still missed Jack so much. I guess I had to accept that he wasn't coming back to me.

CHAPTER TWENTY-FOUR

A COUPLE MORE WEEKS PASSED BY. IT WAS NOW SIX weeks since Jack had left. Alex and I had gone to dinner a couple of times. I even tried surfing again. We spent some afternoons wrapped up in each other, too. Bob was gone pretty often; he was an avid golfer.

One night Alex and I decided to go see a movie. As we were walking up to buy our tickets, Stacy was coming toward us with a grimace on her face. Alex saw her and squeezed my hand harder. I looked up at him feeling a little nervous.

"Hi, Alex. Olivia."

She looked at our hands.

"So, you two are dating, huh? I thought you were with Jack, Olivia? That was a quick change."

"Stacy, there's no need to be rude," said Alex.

"You never called me back. Not even an explanation of why you didn't want to see me anymore. And now you're here with her? Be careful. He is a user." Stacy said with great disdain.

I looked at her and explained. "Stacy, I'm sorry. Alex and I just started hanging out."

Stacy glared at both of us as she walked away. Alex wrapped his arm around me and kissed my forehead.

"Come on. Let's go inside," he said.

"I'm not really feeling like a movie now. Let's just go back to your place," I pleaded.

When we returned to Alex's grandpa's, he made us some tea. He sat down next to me, brushed my hair aside and said, "Are you okay? Sorry about Stacy."

I said, "It's fine. I never told you how horrible she was to me in high school. Some bad feelings came up. That's all."

Alex took my cup of tea, grabbed my hand to pull me up from the couch.

"Let's not talk."

He guided me back to his bedroom.

I was enjoying Alex's company. We got along really well, and he made me laugh. I still thought about Jack but was trying to move on as he clearly had.

October was coming to an end. The days were growing shorter and cooler. Alex told me to dress up because he was picking me up at six. It was a beautiful Sunday afternoon. Fall always hits San Diego a little late. I could see the trees on our street were beginning to change though. The large oak tree in the back of Jack's parent's house was changing, too. It was so beautiful. It was about ten to six. I was sitting in the backyard looking at the trees when I heard the doorbell ring. When I walked inside, I could see my mom opening the door to let Alex inside.

My parents like Alex. Mostly, they were glad that I was happier and smiling more. My mom knew though that most of my heart still belonged to Jack.

"Hi, gorgeous," Alex said as he leaned in to kiss me.

I smiled and said hello.

"You look amazing. Ready to go?"

Tommy came screaming down the stairs just as I was about to say 'yes' and walk out with Alex. He was yelling.

"Jack, Jack! Jack is home!"

I almost threw up. Tommy went running past me flying out the door.

I know I had a shocked look on my face. I looked at Alex. He was staring at me waiting for a reaction.

I didn't know what to say. I think I was shaking a little.

Alex asked, "Do you want to take a rain check? Go see Jack?"

I cleared my throat. "No. Jack doesn't want to see me. Let's go."

As we walked out, I looked over to Jack's house. He was walking slowly to the door. He glanced my way. We made eye contact and then he looked at Alex. Alex waved, but I walked to the car. I could see the disappointment in Jack's face.

Once I was in the car, I saw Tommy hugging Jack and talking nonstop. They disappeared inside the house. Oh how I wished that was me instead of Tommy. I did not know how I would get through the evening. The tone had changed, and Alex knew it. We drove away in silence.

I hardly spoke during the lovely dinner that Alex had taken me to. I was looking down at the crème brulee and just mixing it with my spoon. All I could think was *Jack is back. Jack is back. He didn't even tell me that he was returning.*

"Olivia? Olivia?"

I was jolted out of my trance when Alex touched my hand. I looked up and jumped at the same time.

"I'm sorry to startle you. Are you okay? You're mixing your dessert and off somewhere else." Alex said with a hint of concern in his voice.

I said, "Alex, I'm really sorry. This dinner is wonderful. It was so sweet of you. I know that I am horrible company right now."

Alex looked down at his folded hands on the table. "It's Jack, right? It's okay, Olivia. I know he hurt you. I know how you felt about him."

Just then I looked up at him. Felt? Still feel, I wanted to say. I could see in Alex's face that he knew without me even saying anything. He motioned for the waiter to come over and requested our check. I told Alex I was going to the bathroom and would meet him outside. He stood up before I could and pulled out my chair for me. I wish he wasn't so nice to me. I felt horrible.

We were silent in the car. When we pulled into my driveway, Alex was about to get out, but I touched his arm.

"Alex, thank you for a wonderful dinner. I need to be alone right now. I'm sorry. I hope you understand. I will call you later. Okay?"

Alex leaned over toward me, cupped my face in his hands, and kissed me. It felt like a goodbye kiss. The sort of *I'm sure this is it, so I better get one more in* kind of kiss.

He said, "That's fine. I'll talk to you later."

I waved to him as he drove away. I glanced over at Jack's parents' house. Jack was sitting on the front steps and had seen the whole thing. He dropped his eyes from mine and hung his head. My heart sank. I walked into my house.

Five minutes later, the doorbell rang. I heard my mom open the door. I could only hear muffled noises so wasn't sure who was there. Within seconds, I heard, "Olivia! You have company."

I felt that pit in my stomach. Could it be? It's probably Alex. I must have left something in his car. Yes, that had to be who it was.

I walked slowly down the stairs. There, standing in the entry, was Jack. My heart began to race.

He looked up at me. "Hi, Olivia."

I stopped on the last stair and put my hand on the banister.

"Hello. What do you need?"

My mom was still standing there and felt the tension.

"I will leave you two. Jack, nice to see you."

He smiled at her.

"Olivia, is there somewhere that we can sit and talk?"

"About what, Jack? You have made it pretty clear in these last six weeks that you do not want anything to do with me."

He lowered his eyes then looked back up at me.

"I know that apologizing isn't going to make this better. I would like to explain though. Please?"

I did not want to give him the satisfaction, but I still loved him. I could not just walk away or make him leave.

I agreed to listen. "We can sit in the backyard."

"Thank you," he uttered.

I don't know where my family disappeared to, but no one was in sight. Jack and I walked to the back and sat at the table.

I asked, "Would you like something to drink?"

He replied, "No thanks."

"Well, what do you want to say, Jack?"

"Are you dating Alex?"

"I'm not sure that is any of your business, Jack. You dumped me, remember?"

He looked down. "You're right. It's none of my business. I am just surprised that you have moved on so quickly."

This enraged me. I stood up.

"Are you serious? You dump me. From Paris, nonetheless, won't return my calls or my texts for six weeks. Did you expect me to pine for you until I died? What was I supposed to think, Jack?"

Tears had formed in my eyes and began to stream down my face. Jack stood up and moved towards me.

I put my hand out to stop him.

Jack pleaded. "Olivia, please. I'm sorry. That's not fair. You're right. Please, sit back down. Let me tell you what happened."

Reluctantly, I sat down.

Jack continued. "I'm dying. I didn't think it was fair to keep you when I knew that I wouldn't be around for long. I thought if I ended it, it would be easier."

I interrupted. "For whom? You? Cause it was not easy. Yes, I have been seeing Alex. But, I think about you all of the time. I wonder what I did wrong. I thought you would never return. Although I like Alex, he has just been a distraction for me. I needed to start having some fun again. I couldn't keep working and just returning home to cry myself to sleep."

Jack reached over and grabbed my hand.

"Olivia, I have never stopped loving you. I wanted to protect you, and pushing you away seemed the best plan. Then, once I saw you today, my heart just about leapt out of my chest. I miss you. I don't know how much time I have left, but I want to spend it with you."

I really started crying. He stood up and bent down in front of me. He wrapped his arms around my waist, and I buried my face into his shoulder. I had dreamt of this moment.

I couldn't do it though. I pulled away and pushed him away. Jack looked confused as he stood up.

I stood up. "Jack. I need to think. You really hurt me. I think you should leave."

"Olivia," he pleaded, "I know I hurt you. Please, let me make it up to you. I love you."

"I'm sorry. I need some time."

He walked out reluctantly.

I crumpled back down into the chair, put my head in my hands, and began to sob uncontrollably. Out of nowhere, my mom appeared.

"Olivia. Come here, honey."

We hugged for the longest time. I told her all about Jack's plea. She just listened.

Then when I finished, my mom said, "Olivia, do you love Jack?"

I nodded.

"Do you love Alex?"

I shook my head.

"Olivia, love doesn't come around very often. You don't know how much time Jack has. I know he hurt you, but don't allow pride to keep you from going to him, if that's truly what you want."

She wiped my tears away.

She was right. I didn't want to lose Jack again.

I said, "Thanks, Mom."

I stood up and walked quickly out the front door and over to Jack's. I rang the doorbell. Jack answered.

"Olivia?"

"I love you, Jack. I never stopped loving you."

I fell into his arms, and he closed the door behind us. Jack didn't have his car, so I said that I could take him home. We drove up to his house, and Sumiko met us at the door. She told Jack how happy she was to see him and gave us hugs.

Jack and I spent the night catching up. He wasn't sure if the treatments he had received in Paris were going to work. For the time being, he was feeling alright. He knew though that the treatments would just prolong his life and probably not guarantee anything else. He apologized profusely all night. I easily slipped back into his arms and the comfort of his company. I had missed him so deeply.

I kept hearing my phone chiming during the night, but did not check it until the morning. It had been Alex texting and calling.

His one voicemail said: *Olivia. I know that you are feeling confused. I won't say anything about Jack because I think he is a good guy. I will say though that you need to be honest with me. I have fallen for you over these few weeks and need*

to know if there is any hope of us continuing all of the fun that
we have been having. Please call me.

I pushed delete.

Jack startled me. "Morning, Alex calling?"

I was embarrassed. "Yes. I should go see him and explain."

"Do you have to see him?"

I looked at Jack like *really*?

He said, "Okay. Do what you need to do."

"I'll call you later. I need to go the office, too."

We kissed a very long kiss. Then I left.

I was grinning again. It felt like a dream. Then, I felt queasy at the thought of telling Alex that I was not going to continue seeing him.

CHAPTER TWENTY-FIVE

WENT HOME TO CHANGE AND THEN WENT STRAIGHT TO the office. I was supposed to meet Mrs. Heart at one. When I walked into the office, my mom caught my eye and motioned for me to enter her office.

"Good morning, Mom," I said as I plopped onto her couch.

"Well, good morning. How's everything?"

I was grinning ear to ear.

"Wonderful. It's as if he didn't break my heart six weeks ago."

My mom placed her hands on her desk and leaned forward. "That concerns me, honey. I really don't want your heart broken again. It was very hard to watch."

"I know, Mom. I don't either. I never stopped loving him or hoping that he would change his mind. I am nervous to talk to Alex, but know that I need to do that very soon."

I worked for a little bit and then left for Mrs. Heart's around twelve. Alex text messaged me a couple of times. I needed to call him.

When I got into my car, I dialed Alex.

He answered with a hint of hope in his voice.

"Olivia, Hi."

"Hi, Alex. How are you?"

"I'm well. I was hoping to hear from you. Can we meet? I think we should talk."

"Yes. We do need to talk. I should be finished with work around four. Do you want to meet at Starbucks?"

"I would rather meet at my gramp's. Is that okay?"

I was nervous about that choice. I responded after a slight pause.

"Um, I guess that's okay. I will see you around four thirty depending on the traffic."

"Okay. Looking forward to seeing you."

I hung up knowing that Jack wouldn't be thrilled about me going to Alex's house. I also felt that Jack didn't have much say in this.

As soon as I walked into Mrs. Heart's, she took one look at me and said, "Oh dear, this calls for tea."

I said, "How do you know?"

She just smiled at me and motioned for me to sit down. Over tea, I told her what had happened. She took a sip of her tea, put her cup down, and grabbed my hands.

"Olivia, I know that you feel badly about Alex. He's a wonderful man and been a good distraction for you. Who knows how long you have with Jack. I know you love him deeply. Don't waste any more time."

I smiled. "I won't. I won't."

I was on my way to see Alex when my phone rang. It was Jack.

"Hello, beautiful. I hope you are on your way to my place soon."

"Hi, Jack. I need to take care of something and then will be there, okay?"

"Okay. What are you doing? Lots of work to finish?"

I paused. "Um, no. I'm on my way to speak to Alex."

There was silence on the other end.

"Jack, are you there?"

"Yes. I'm here. Where are you meeting him?"

Great. Here it goes.

"I'm just going to Bob's house. I won't be long okay? I will call you when I'm on my way to your house. I'm almost to Bob's now. I'm sure he is there, too, so don't worry. I love you."

Jack paused again. "Okay. I can't wait to see you."

I pulled into Bob's house and only saw Alex's car. *Great,* I thought.

I knocked on the door. Alex answered with a grin on his face. He pulled me close to him and hugged me. I hugged him back but not in a romantic way. He could sense my distance.

We walked into the living room, and there were two glasses of wine on the coffee table.

Alex said, "I thought you might like a glass of red. I know you have had a long day."

I sat down. "I guess one glass is okay. Alex, let me start, okay?"

He sat next to me, handed a glass of wine to me, and clinked my glass. "Cheers!" He said and took a sip.

I sipped my wine.

"Alex."

He placed two fingers on my mouth and interrupted

me. "Olivia, I have missed you. I have fallen for you in the last few weeks."

He leaned in and began kissing me. I pulled away.

"Alex, I can't. I came here to tell you that we can't see each other anymore. I love Jack. You know that I always have."

Alex sat back. "I guess I was hoping that you were having too much fun with me. Jack hurt you really bad. Do you remember that?"

"Yes, of course I do. He knows how badly he hurt me and is sorry. He's sick. He did it for my own good. Alex, I do like you. I have had so much fun. It's just that, well, I'm in love with Jack."

He looked at me.

"I think you should give it a little time. He just returned and you're just going to forgive him just like that? Well, I'm sorry but I cannot be here for you the next time you fall apart. I can't take that, Olivia. I have liked you ever since I laid eyes on you. I will have to distance myself. Sorry."

I put down my half drunken glass of wine. I told him I understood and was sorry. I stood up to leave and turned to find Alex right behind me.

Alex asked, "One last kiss goodbye?"

I thought it couldn't hurt. Jack didn't need to know. Alex leaned in after I gave him the nod of approval. He kissed me so deeply; my knees became weak. I had to pull away.

"Goodbye. I hope we can be friends after a while."

"Goodbye, Olivia."

In the thirty minutes I had been at Alex's, Jack had texted twice. It annoyed me. I texted him that I was on my way to his house.

When I pulled up to Jack's house, it was almost six. My stomach was growling. I walked inside and found Jack on the back deck.

"Hi, babe," I said as I approached him.

He turned around and stood up. He pulled me so close and buried his face into my neck.

"Hello, beautiful. I'm so glad you are here."

Sumiko had prepared a delicious dinner for us, and Jack had a bottle of red open. He didn't ask about Alex. I was relieved but thought I needed to let him know how annoyed I was at him texting so much. I decided to tell him later. We ate dinner and talked into the evening.

We were cleaning up the dishes from dinner and Jack said we should talk about our future. The lightness of the evening just became very heavy. It was if a black cloud settled in over our heads. I stopped washing dishes and said, "Okay. Should we sit down?"

Jack grabbed my hand and walked me into the living room. "I have an appointment tomorrow to find out if the treatments worked. I was hoping that you could go with me."

I hugged him and said, "Of course. I want to be by your side. We will figure this out together."

"Olivia, don't get your hopes up. It might not have worked at all."

I just smiled at him.

"Jack, you came back to me. I have hope."

The next morning, Jack and I drove to the doctor's appointment. It was much cooler outside now as we were entering November.

My palms were sweaty as we sat waiting for the doctor. Jack and I weren't talking. We were both nervous. Jack grabbed my hand and just then the door opened. It jarred both of us.

"Hi, Jack. You must be Olivia."

I stood up and shook the doc's hand.

"Yes, hi. It's nice to meet you."

The doctor stood behind his desk with his hands on top of a file that read "Jack Fall, Medical Records." Jack's hands were sweating.

"Doctor Stein, please. I can't take the suspense. Did it work or should I start planning my funeral?"

I slapped Jack lightly on the shoulder.

"Not funny."

Dr. Stein said, "Not yet, Jack. It seems the treatments in Paris have stopped the growth of the tumor in your lungs. It shrunk a little even."

I started to cry. I couldn't believe my ears. Jack squeezed my hand tighter, and I could see tears welling up in his eyes too. Jack could barely talk.

"Stein, really? Maybe I should go back for more treatments. If it worked, maybe it will shrink the whole thing."

Stein shook his head. "No, Jack. Your body could not handle that again right now. You need to rest. Eat healthy. Enjoy life. We will scan you again in a month to see what is happening. Until then, use the oxygen as needed. Questions?"

Jack and I were silent as we walked out to his car. Once we were both inside the car, we hugged for the longest time.

"Jack, this is amazing news. I'm so happy."

"Me too, Olivia. Me too."

Although I knew he was happy, I sensed some concern in his voice.

"What is it?" I said.

Jack brushed the hair away from my eye and smiled. "Nothing. Nothing."

I decided to work from Jack's. I didn't want to be away from him.

CHAPTER TWENTY-SIX

Two Months Later

I WOKE UP TO SOME CLANGING IN THE KITCHEN. IT startled me since the last I knew Jack was upstairs. I got up and called out.

"Jack? Is that you?"

I walked down the hallway into the kitchen. There was Jack rummaging through a drawer.

"Jack, what are you doing?"

He jumped. "Oh, you scared me. I'm just hungry. I'm looking for a small pot for some soup."

"Why don't you let me make it for you?"

I walked over to him and took the pot. I grabbed some chicken noodle from the pantry.

"Sit down. I can do this. Can I get you something to drink? 7Up?"

Jack sat down at the bar. He put his head into his hands and rubbed his face.

"Yes, that sounds good."

"Are you okay?" I said, feeling concerned. "Are you nauseous?"

Jack said he just felt rundown. I turned on the stove to heat up his soup. I put the glass of 7Up in front of him and sat down next to him and rubbed his back.

After he finished his soup, he went back to bed. It was only about eight, so I poured a glass of wine and turned on a movie. I had dozed off during the movie and woke up on the couch. I had no idea what time it was. I grabbed my phone and saw that it was two in the morning. I slipped off the couch and headed up to our room. When I walked in, he wasn't there. I saw the bathroom light on. Then I heard it. He was throwing up. I knocked lightly on the door.

"Jack, can I help?"

He heaved one more time.

"No. It's okay. Maybe you should sleep in the guest room tonight. I'll call you, if I need anything."

"Okay, I'm so sorry."

I grabbed my pajamas and went to one of the other bedrooms. I crawled into bed and was asleep right as my head hit the pillow.

I woke up early the next morning since I was worried about Jack. I crawled out of bed and went into the bathroom to wash my face. I could hear voices coming from the hallway. I slipped on a sweater and opened my door. I stepped out into the hallway and headed toward our bedroom. I saw Sumiko standing in our bedroom doorway.

"Good morning, Sumiko."

She turned around quickly. "Oh, Ms. Olivia, morning. I didn't hear you coming."

"How is Jack this morning?"

She stepped aside and let me enter. I walked in to find

Jack laying in bed still. I sat down next him.

"How are you today?"

He looked pale and said he'd been awake most of the night. He apologized for being bad company.

"Jack, you don't need to apologize. Rest today. I'll be here as soon as I'm finished with work, okay?"

He nodded. I leaned in and kissed him on the forehead. I walked out and told Sumiko to take good care of him. I showered and got ready for work. I had enough clothes at Jack's now that I didn't need to go home.

When I walked into the office, I filled my coffee cup and went to my mom's office. I sat down on her comfy couch. She was on the phone, so I sipped my coffee and waited for her to finish.

"Hi honey. How are you? How's Jack?"

Tears came to my eyes, and she walked over to sit next to me.

"Not good, huh?" She said.

I shook my head and told her about my night.

"Mom, I really thought the Paris treatment was going to do it. Stein seemed hopeful especially since the scan two weeks ago was fine. When Jack started feeling sick last week, I wanted to ignore it. I just don't want to believe that I could lose him."

I started crying, and my mom hugged me.

"I'm sorry, Olivia. I don't know what to say. We all want Jack to beat this."

I composed myself after a few minutes. I didn't linger as I had a lot of work to do. I didn't get to Jack's until six. I had texted Sumiko and asked her to stay until I arrived. She was waiting in the foyer when I opened the door. I thanked her for staying and asked where Jack was. She said he was sitting out on the patio and had a good day. She walked out and said she'd see me in the morning.

I put down my things and walked outside.

"Hi, sweetie," I said as I approached Jack.

He looked over and smiled at me.

"Hey, there. Have a seat."

I sat down on the couch next to him. The fire pit was roaring and there was a glass of red on the table.

"I guess you're feeling better, huh?" I asked pointing to the wine.

"That's for you. I knew you were on your way, so I thought you might like some wine."

I picked up the glass and took a sip. It did taste very good after the day I had. I scooted in next to him. He told me that he slept a lot and was feeling better.

I laid my head on his shoulder and stared at the flames jumping around in the night air. After an hour, we decided to go to bed. I tossed and turned all night. I kept dreaming about Alex and Stacy. They were both laughing and pointing at me. I woke up all sweaty. Jack turned over and saw me.

"Are you okay? You tossed and turned all night. You're sweating profusely, too."

I got out of bed. I told him I was just having bad dreams and then got into the shower. My eyes were closed as the shampoo ran out of my hair. I heard the shower door open. Before I knew it, Jack was up against me kissing my neck.

I said, "Well, I guess someone is feeling better."

It was good to have him back. I forgot all about that dream. We were getting dressed and Jack said he was feeling up to working and wondered if I was going to the office as well. I told him I had a busy day with Mrs. Heart's project. I slipped on my dress and stepped into my heels.

While I was getting ready, I had that dream on my mind. I hadn't heard from Alex since I left his grandpa's house. I had sent him a "Happy Thanksgiving" text, but no response. I grabbed my purse and work bag.

"Well, I gotta go to work."

I walked over to Jack, hugged and kissed him, and started to walk away.

Jack said, "Olivia? Are you okay?"

Crap. He sensed it.

I turned around. "Yes. Why?"

He said, "I don't know. You just seem a little off. Never mind. See you for dinner?"

I walked over to kiss and hug him again.

"Yes! Definitely see you for dinner. Have a great day! Love you."

He said he loved me, too, and I left.

I really need to stop this stuff about Alex. I don't even want to be with him. I did wonder how he was doing. I wanted him to be happy.

CHAPTER TWENTY-SEVEN

I HAD WORKED FOR A COUPLE OF HOURS WHEN I DECIDED to call Jack. I hadn't even heard my phone but noticed two missed calls from Jack. Somehow my phone had been placed on silent. I listened to the voicemail:

Hey, beautiful! I hope you're having a wonderful day. I'm going to pick you up at your office around five. Let me know if that won't work. Call me back!

I called Jack back, and he told me he had a surprise for me. He wouldn't even give me a hint. I just had to be ready to go at five. It was four so I kept working until a quarter to five then freshened up.

The door opened and in walked Jack with a dozen stargazer lilies. I thought *this man is amazing*. I smiled, stood up, and hugged him.

"Thank you. They are beautiful."

He placed the vase on my desk.

"I thought you needed some flowers here, too. Ready?"

I grabbed my purse and coat.

"Yes, very ready."

Stacy was coming in as we were heading out. I hadn't seen her since the encounter with Alex. I told Jack I would be right out. I stopped Stacy and said we should talk. She agreed. She apologized for being so rude. I told her I was sorry, too. I assured her that I didn't know Alex had not called her back to explain. She asked about Jack, and I told her how happy I was that he was back. We wished each other well, and I walked out.

There was a black limo waiting right outside the office. He still wouldn't tell me where we were headed. We drove around for a little while and then I noticed we were driving toward Mission Bay. We pulled into Paradise Point, which was one of my favorite spots in San Diego. The limo dropped us off near the lobby to the hotel.

I asked excitedly, "Are we staying here tonight?"

He shook his head. "No, just eating dinner."

He took my hand and led me to the back of the property. Right on the beach next to a fire pit was a beautiful table all set for dinner. We walked the path on the sand lined with candles that led us to the table. Jack pulled out my chair for me. I sat down and sunk my toes into the sand under the table.

"Jack, this is so amazing."

The moon was shining on the rippling bay. A waiter was standing off in the near distance ready to serve any request. Not far from our table was a fire pit that was sending embers up into the night sky. It was like a dream.

We ate dinner under the stars and shared so many laughs. It was good to see Jack feeling better again. It was the middle of December now and the nights were still warm.

The waiter delivered my favorite dessert: crème brulee. I smiled at Jack, and he knew he had done well. Just as I was finishing the crème brulee, Jack stood up, walked over next to me, and dropped to his knees. My heart leapt. What was he doing? Proposing?

He grabbed my hands.

"Olivia, I have never loved someone like I love you. I know I want to be with you for as long as I have on earth."

He reached into his pocket and pulled out a black velvet box. He opened it to reveal the most brilliant diamond ring. It was at least two carats.

"Olivia, will you do me the honor of becoming my wife?"

Immediately tears filled my eyes. I instinctively held out my left hand.

"Yes, yes, of course!"

He slipped the ring onto my finger; it was a perfect fit. We both stood up and hugged and kissed. The waiter started clapping, which made both of us chuckle. We had forgotten that we weren't alone. We walked over to the fire and sat in the Adirondack chairs and started planning our future. While sitting next to the fire, we decided to have a fall wedding. Even though it was ten months away, we were hopeful that Jack was on the mend. Although I could have sat there the whole night, it was getting late, so the limo dropped us off at the office because I had to get my car. Jack stayed with me, and we started to drive back to his house. I was in a daze. I was incredibly happy and couldn't believe what was happening.

Suddenly I realized that I wanted to tell my parents. "Jack, we need to stop at my house. We need to tell my parents."

He agreed, and I drove to my house.

When we got there, my parents were sitting in the living room with a bottle of champagne. I looked at Jack.

"They knew?"

He said, "Of course! You think I would propose without asking your parents' permission?"

I walked over and hugged both of them. My dad opened the champagne. Just then Tommy came down the stairs.

He rubbed his sleepy eyes while saying, "What's going on? Oh, hey, Jack."

I held out my hand to show him the ring. I was nervous to see his reaction. To my surprise, Tommy ran over and hugged both of us.

He said, "Yes! I always wanted to have a brother."

We all laughed. My mom grabbed some sparkling apple juice so Tommy could toast with us. That was one of the happiest nights of my life.

CHAPTER TWENTY-EIGHT

A COUPLE OF WEEKS HAD GONE BY SINCE I HAD become engaged. I was walking on air. Jack was feeling pretty good. Jack and I had decided on an October wedding. We hadn't finalized the date yet but knew it would be in his backyard. He has the perfect party house. We didn't want anything too big though.

Jack was feeling pretty good but did get tired quickly. He went to sleep early one night, so I closed his door and went downstairs to get something to eat. While my food was warming in the microwave my phone chimed. I looked down thinking it would be Jack. It was a text from Alex. My stomach was in knots as I opened it.

Hey, Olivia. How are you? It's been awhile since we've talked or even seen each other. Are you free to get coffee some- time soon?

I put down the phone. I wasn't sure about seeing him. I knew we were just friends, but I still felt strange about it. I guess meeting for coffee wouldn't hurt. I picked up my phone and texted him back and said I was free for coffee tomorrow. We agreed to meet at nine the next morning at Starbucks.

I checked on Jack before heading to bed. I slept in the other room so he could have the bed to himself. I heard him get up around two in the morning. No doubt he was sick. I climbed out of bed to check on him. He was back in bed sleeping.

The next morning I got ready and went to say goodbye to Jack. He was lying in bed reading the paper when I entered. He folded the paper back to look at me.

"You're up early."

"Morning. I have an early meeting. I need to get going. Get some rest and I'll see you for dinner."

I kissed him and walked out the door.

I looked around for Alex when I walked into Starbucks but didn't see him. I stepped into line to order some coffee when I felt arms wrap around my waist. I turned around and there he was.

"Hi, Alex."

We hugged. He smelled really good.

"I just arrived. What would you like? My treat."

He insisted that he pay since he had invited me. I succumbed.

We sat down in the corner in some comfy chairs. I grabbed my coffee and took a sip. I saw Alex's eyes double in size. I had forgotten that he didn't know about the engagement.

"Olivia! What is that?" He pointed at my ring.

"Uh, oh yes. That. Jack proposed a couple of weeks ago."

"A couple of weeks? Why didn't you tell me?"

"I'm telling you now. Life has been busy. I haven't had a lot of time. Sorry."

"Well, when's the big day?"

"We are thinking late October."

"Next October, right?" He said with a hint of judgment.

"Well, no. This October."

"Wow. Why the rush? Oh, because Jack is sick? Do you really think that's the best choice, Olivia?"

I was beginning to feel annoyed. Who was he to judge the decisions that Jack and I were making? Yes, he was sick, but we also knew that we wanted to be together so why wait.

"Alex, I don't think I need to explain anything to you. I just want you to be happy for me. If you can't, then I should just go."

I started to get up, but Alex touched my hand.

"Wait. I'm sorry. You're right. I'm just surprised. Sit down. Tell me about it."

I told him our plans. He told me he was dating a little, but no one measured up to me. Of course that stroked my ego a bit, okay a lot, but I just gave him a smile and flashed my ring. At ten, I said I needed to get to work. We walked out together and hugged before we parted.

I only stayed at work until two. I wanted to see Jack and figured I could do some work at his house. When I pulled in, I noticed Jon's car was parked in the driveway. As I walked inside, I could see through the windows in the living room that Jack and Jon were sitting outside on the patio. Jack saw me and motioned for me to join them.

Jon got up and hugged me. I walked over and kissed Jack.

"Hi, beautiful, have a seat. Join us."

"I will. How are you, Jon? Haven't seen you in awhile."

"I'm well. I just saw you this morning though."

I looked at Jack and back at Jon.

"You did? Where?"

"I was pulling up to Starbucks and saw you and Alex walking out together."

My cheeks became very warm. Jack looked at me.

"I thought you had an early meeting?"

I cleared my throat.

"I did. It was with Alex. We were just wrapping up some things from his grandpa's project."

Crap. I felt like Jon was looking right through me. He was trying to catch me at something that was nothing.

Jack asked, "Oh. How is he doing?"

I could sense some annoyance in his voice. I should have told him. Of course the project had been finished for awhile.

I smiled and said, "He's fine."

Jon said, "Oh. Hmm. Well, I'm off."

I felt like he had come here to "tell" on me. I couldn't meet Alex anymore. I couldn't take any chances.

Jack and I walked Jon out. We both hugged him good-bye. Jack turned to me, grabbed my hand, and we walked back inside. I felt that Jack wanted to say something to me about my having met with Alex. I turned to him and asked if he was okay.

Jack faced me and claimed, "Olivia. If you are going to be my wife, you have to be honest with me. Although I am jealous of Alex, I know that you worked on his grandpa's house. I actually really like Alex. You know that. Just be honest, okay?"

I hugged him and said that I was sorry.

It was pretty early in the day. I needed to do a little work, and Jack was tired. He went upstairs and I sat down with my computer.

I felt bad about lying to Jack. There wasn't anything going on, but it would seem like it if I had to lie. There's no reason Jack needs to know anything. I think Jon believed me. I worked for a couple of hours. Sumiko had made dinner again, which was really nice. Jack came down to eat with me.

When we sat down to eat, I looked at him and realized he didn't have his oxygen tube in.

Dr. Stein told Jack to try and go without once in awhile. He seemed to be doing pretty well. About ten minutes had passed when he started to wheeze a little. We looked at each other and both knew. Jack grabbed the tube and placed it into his nose. I looked at him feeling sad.

He smiled, but I knew he was just as disappointed as I was. I was worried. I couldn't help it. I couldn't escape the foreboding feeling. The next morning I had to go to Mrs. Heart's again. I was feeling pretty sad about Jack not being able to go too long without his oxygen.

I had a lot to do. Jack had asked me to move in with him so I was busy with work and packing my stuff at night. I really didn't have much so it wouldn't be too difficult. I was going to Mrs. Heart's and then home to get some of my clothes.

When I arrived to Mrs. Heart's place, she was not very happy. Apparently, the paint color in the kitchen wasn't what she had expected. She made the painter cease his painting until I arrived. I sat her down and calmed her. I told her that I would make sure to get the color she wanted. Once she was calm, she apologized to everyone for freaking out.

After leaving Mrs. Heart's, I headed home to grab some clothes. When I arrived to Jack's, he was sitting in the living room. He got up to greet me and led me upstairs. He said he had a surprise for me. He led me into the closet, and I couldn't believe my eyes. A beautiful crystal chandelier was hanging in the center of the closet over the island that served as a space for my jewelry. There were new pairs of shoes, dresses, jeans, beautiful tops and a few new handbags. I looked at Jack finally.

"Jack, this is a-amazing. I don't know what to say."

He hugged me.

"Say you love it. Say you love me."

I hugged him and whispered into his ear.

"Jack, I love and adore you and LOVE this closet. Thank you. I can't wait to marry you.

He took my face into his hands.

"What are we waiting for? Let's get married!"

I said, "What do you mean? We are getting married."

He said, "Let's get married this weekend."

I couldn't believe what I was hearing.

"Really?" I asked.

"Really," Jack said.

We kissed.

"Let's do it. What are we waiting for?"

I was elated!

It was Wednesday, so we needed to get planning.

CHAPTER TWENTY-NINE

On Friday, I went to Mrs. Heart's. She was happier this time. Her place was looking great. I got a whim to invite her to the wedding. She seemed like she could use a party. I know she was still grieving her husband's death. To my surprise, she said she would love to go. She and I had grown pretty close during her remodel.

Saturday was spent getting everything ready. The amount of flowers that were arriving took my breath away. Beautiful lights were going up over the patio and throughout the trees. People were busy in the kitchen preparing the food. There was going to be about 50 people. I had invited Alex and his grandpa to attend, and they said they would.

After checking on everything, I decided to go upstairs. I was looking for Jack. I heard some noise coming from the bathroom. It almost sounded like a cat trying to cough up a fur ball. The door was slightly ajar so I peeked in.

"Jack? Are you in there?"

"I'm here. I'm not feeling too well. Give me a minute. I'll be back downstairs soon."

I was concerned.

"Are you sure you don't need me?"

"No, Olivia. I'm fine. Really."

His tone was a bit sharp. That ominous feeling crept into my mind and heart again. I was scared.

About ten minutes later, Jack appeared in the doorway of the kitchen. I was glad to see him.

"Hi, are you okay?"

He was coughing pretty hard. He managed to get a reprieve.

"Yes. Just an annoying cough. I wonder if I am coming down with something."

Jack said he wanted to take a nap before the company arrived. We were having our families over for a pre-wedding dinner. It was a rehearsal dinner, I guess, although no rehearsing was happening. It was going to be a very simple ceremony with Jack and me at the altar.

At five, I woke up Jack. He was still a little groggy, but I coaxed him out of bed with a *let's take a shower together* proposition. He couldn't resist. He was awake within seconds!

At six, the family began to arrive. We had the dinner catered so we could just enjoy everyone's company. Jack had hired one of my favorites: True Food.

I could tell that Jack still wasn't feeling up to par, but he was hiding it pretty well from the others. We mingled for a little while and then sat down to dinner.

My mom asked if everything was ready. I told her we just needed the cake to arrive.

Tommy asked where we were going for our honeymoon. Jack told him it was a surprise.

I knew it would have to be somewhere pretty close by.

Jack's doctor requested that he not travel too far. We didn't want another incident like Napa. I was very curious what he was going to come up with. I guess I would find out Monday morning.

Everyone stayed until about ten. All of us were pretty tired, but mostly Jack. They all said their goodbyes, and we went to bed.

I crawled under the blankets and nuzzled up against Jack. He put his arm around me, and I fell asleep on his shoulder tucked under his chin.

The next morning when I woke up, Jack wasn't in bed so

I walked downstairs to look for him. When I walked through the foyer, I could see to the back patio. There he was sitting next to the fire pit. A relief filled my body as I walked outside.

"There you are. I was looking for you."

I sat down next to him. He wrapped his arm around me. He said, "I was feeling a little cold but wanted to be outside so I lit the fire. Isn't it a beautiful day?"

I leaned deeper into his body.

"Yes, Jack. Yes, it is."

We sat there silent for quite some time. We were enjoying the peace and quietness of the property. Although there were workers busy around us, we seemed to be encased in our own tight bubble. I never wanted this moment to end. I was so in love at that moment. I felt love and safety. Jack started to cough and the reality of Jack's sickness reared its ugly head again. Just like that, the bubble popped.

I dozed off on the couch in front of the warm fire and

my dreams tortured me. I kept finding myself in a cemetery. I was standing in front of a gravestone, which had Jack's name on it. Someone put their hand on my shoulder. When I turned around, it was Jack. I woke up suddenly and remembered where I was.

I got up and went into the house. Sumiko met us in the kitchen with breakfast. She was busy, too, so Jack and I sat down and ate together while the whirlwind circled around us.

After breakfast, I went upstairs to shower. I was going to have my hair and makeup done at two. The ceremony was at four. I told Jack that he was not allowed to see me again until the ceremony.

At 3:45, I slipped into my Vera Wang wedding dress. It was simple yet so elegant. My mom and dad walked into the bedroom. They both looked at me with tears in their eyes.

My mom gasped. "Oh, Olivia. You make a beautiful bride. I'm so happy for you."

Dad hugged me and whispered into my ear.

"You look beautiful, honey."

I wasn't crying, surprisingly. I stood between them, put my arm in theirs, and asked, "Ready?"

We walked down the stairs. I could see our guests sitting down waiting for me. Sumiko motioned to the DJ. My music began. I walked towards Jack to the traditional "Here Comes the Bride." I was grinning ear to ear. Jack looked so handsome standing there waiting for me under the arbor covered in white peonies. My florist special ordered them for me. There were also some green vines intertwined in the peonies. Jack was smiling and took my hand.

"Hello, beautiful."

I smiled at him. We walked forward together and said our vows. Jack managed to refrain from coughing during the ceremony, but I could tell it was a challenge for him.

Jon had gone online and gotten his marital license so he was marrying us. We turned toward each other and began our vows.

Jack spoke first.

"Olivia. The moment I saw you on my deck I felt a pull towards you. Your warm smile and kind heart have seeped their way into my soul. I promise to love and cherish you for the rest of my life. I promise to stand by your side and always be there for any rough times. I'm yours and you're mine. I can't believe you have agreed to be my wife. There are no more gloomy days now that you are by my side. I love you."

Tears filled my eyes. Jack dabbed the tears away with his handkerchief. It was my turn.

"Jack. Words cannot explain the love that I have for you, but I will try. The moment I had that first glance of you when you were at your parents' house, I knew I wanted to know you. Your kind spirit and giving nature have completely engulfed me. I long to be by your side when I am not. I promise to love you for the rest of my life. I promise to support you in good times and bad. I will love you in sickness and health. I promise to gaze at the stars each evening with you as we sit by the fire. I love you now and will love you forever. I am yours and you are mine."

Tears continued down my cheeks and Jack wiped them away. He leaned in for a quick kiss.

Jon teased, "Ah ah ah, it's not time yet!"

The guests laughed.

When the ceremony was over, we joined our guests for an amazing party. As the sun set, the lights hanging in the trees and above the patio twinkled over us. There were also candles scattered around the tables, which was so romantic. The center pieces on the tables rose up like big wine glasses and had white flowers flowing over the edges. It was a dream. We had a delicious dinner and then the dancing began. Jack was able to complete the first dance but then sat down. I danced with my dad, which is when some tears came to my eyes. After that, almost everyone took to the dance floor.

During dinner Jack and I made rounds saying hello to our guests. I made my way over to Alex and his grandpa. I sat Mrs. Heart at the same table as them hoping they would like one another. As I walked over, I could see Bob and Mrs. Heart having what seemed to be an intimate conversation. They were both leaning in toward one another. They were either hitting it off, or perhaps they just couldn't hear one another!

The chair next to Alex was empty so I sat down.

"Hi, Alex. Thank you for coming."

"Olivia. You look gorgeous. I'm happy for you."

Just then Bob interrupted. "Olivia. You're a vision."

He leaned down to kiss me on the cheek.

"Thank you, Bob. I'm so glad you made it. I see you have met Mrs. Heart."

I walked over and hugged her.

"I'm so glad you made it."

151

Mrs. Heart said, "I'm glad to be here. It's been nice getting to know Bob, too."

I smiled and told them all to enjoy the party.

Just then Alex stood up and asked if he could dance with me. I was hesitant but decided it would be okay. As we walked toward the dance floor, Jack was watching us. He smiled at me, but it felt uncomfortable. Alex took me in his arms, and we began to dance.

Alex placed his cheek against mine and whispered. "There will always be an ember burning in me for you, Olivia. I wish it was me standing up front with you."

This made me very uncomfortable. I pulled away though still continued to dance.

"Alex, I'm a married woman now. We have to have boundaries. I appreciate your kind words, but we can only be friends."

I saw Jack staring at us. His expression was not a happy one. Then he started walking toward us. My heart raced. Jack tapped Alex on the shoulder.

"Alex, mind if I cut in with my beautiful wife?"

Alex stepped aside.

"Of course not."

Jack grabbed me around the waist, leaned in to my ear, and whispered. "He was a little too close to my wife."

I kissed Jack on the cheek. "Thanks for rescuing me."

I watched Alex mosey back over to the bar. He smelled of alcohol already so he was definitely tying one on for the night.

After the dance, I continued to walk around greeting our guests while Jack sat back down. I could tell he was struggling a bit and needed his oxygen.

I walked back to Jack, sat next to him, and grabbed his hand. We smiled at one another.

"Hello, wife," he said.

I smiled and said, "Hello, husband."

Just then there was a crash. We jerked our heads around to see Alex on the floor. He jumped up quickly and started brushing himself off. His grandpa raced over to him.

"Alex, are you okay? Maybe you should slow down on the beer," Bob said with concern.

Alex pushed him away. "I'm fine, gramps! Just enjoying my evening."

Alex stumbled back to his seat where I could see his grandpa trying to talk to him.

I told Jack that I should go talk to him. Jack wasn't thrilled with that but agreed. I walked over to Alex and told him to follow me.

Alex winked at his table mates. "Oh, now the bride wants me."

We walked into the foyer. I turned around to see Alex right behind me. He grabbed me around the waist and pulled me in tightly.

"Alex, stop. I think you should go. You have had too much to drink, and you're going to embarrass yourself."

Then, he tried to kiss me. I pushed him away.

"Stop it!"

Just then someone pulled him away. It was Jon.

"Alex, let's get you some water."

"Oh hey, Jon, Olivia was just 'talking' to me." He quoted the air.

I looked at Jon and mouthed, *Thank you.*

Just beyond the backdoor was Jack. He motioned for me to go to him. I walked over, and he took me in his arms. Alex's grandpa intervened and took Alex home. He exchanged numbers with Mrs. Heart, too. My plan had worked!

Most of the people were gone by ten. Jack and I made our way to the dance floor one more time before calling it a night.

CHAPTER THIRTY

MOST PEOPLE THINK A NEWLY MARRIED COUPLE will stay up all night making love. This was not the case for us. We were both so exhausted by the time the last guest left that we both practically fell into bed.

We slept as late as possible the next day. Jack said I needed to be ready by ten because a limo was picking us up to begin our honeymoon. He still wouldn't tell me where we were going, but I didn't care as long as I was with him. He seemed to be feeling okay that morning. I hoped he had just caught a bug or something and was now on the mend. He had a doctor's appointment the week after we would return from our trip. We agreed to not talk *sickness* on our trip.

Just as we were about to leave, I received a text from Alex:

Olivia, I'm so sorry for my behavior last night. Clearly, I have unresolved feelings for you. I'm very happy for you and Jack though. Please tell him that I'm embarrassed and sorry. Enjoy your honeymoon.

Jack saw me focusing on my phone and asked if I was okay. I replied that I was just reading the apology text from Alex.

Jack scoffed. "Well, I think it's best to not be in touch with him anymore."

I wasn't happy about Jack denying my friendship with Alex. Even though he had embarrassed me at the wedding, I understood. I agreed though so Jack would feel better.

Our first stop was Santa Barbara. We stayed in a beautiful hotel right on the beach. The plan was to stay there for a couple of nights, do some wine tasting, and sightseeing. I had always wanted to see the Hearst Castle so Jack took me there. He could walk around but had to take it slow.

After Santa Barbara, we drove up to Carmel. Carmel is such a cute quaint town. I love it there. We stayed in a little hotel that had rooms that were separate cottages; it was so delightful. In the mornings, when I would run, the fog was still crawling over the streets. By noon each day, the sun was out. We stayed in Carmel for two nights.

On our last night in Carmel, we went to dinner, and I could tell Jack had something on his mind.

"Jack, are you okay? You seem distant?"

He grabbed my hand across the table and smiled.

"I'm okay. I don't want our honeymoon to end. I know we said we would not talk about the "sickness' but it just seems like the elephant in the room. I'm scared that I may leave you alone. I want you to know that you will be well taken care should anything happen to me."

My eyes welled. "Jack, I can't think about that. We have to remain positive. It's good to plan, but it just worries me."

He grabbed my hand a little tighter. "I know, my love. I know."

The rest of the night was a bit more solemn. We decided

to go into our private Jacuzzi when we went back to the hotel. Jack was staring at me.

"What?" I asked.

Jack said, "Nothing. I'm just admiring your beauty. You know, we don't need our suits on."

He inched toward me and scooped me up in his arms. He reached behind and untied my bikini top.

I whispered into his ear. "Mr. Fall, what are you up to?"

He kissed my neck and whispered back. "Mrs. Fall, stop talking. I'm trying to seduce you. Maybe we should dry off and go to our bed."

I grabbed his face with my hands, kissed him, and said, "I think we should just stay here."

We easily sunk into each other and made love right there in the Jacuzzi.

The next morning we enjoyed some breakfast on our patio and then began the drive back to San Diego. I was elated. It had been a wonderful trip, but now back to reality.

CHAPTER THIRTY-ONE

October

MOTHER NATURE HAD SPLASHED HER VIBRANT colors onto the leaves of the trees in what seemed like overnight. We were coming up on 8 months of marriage. Unfortunately, a melancholy mood had set in. Jack became sick when we returned from our honeymoon. We had hoped it was just the flu, but the cancer had returned. Jack had fought hard, but nothing was working. He was getting sicker with each passing day. Fall was quickly becoming my least favorite season as all it represented to me now was death. My love's slow death.

We decided to have our family over for a nice dinner since we weren't sure how long Jack had.

The table looked beautiful. I had the florist emulate the centerpieces from our wedding. The lights were hanging above the table and throughout the trees.

Jack spent most of his days sleeping now. He was weaker every day. I could hardly stand to witness him slipping away from me. It wasn't fair. I met the love of my life and now he was being taken, stolen away from me. I had gone from elated and loving life a year ago to wishing I could slip away and never come up for air again.

I had the dinner catered so we could all enjoy ourselves. Sumiko was there, too; she was part of our family. I often heard her crying in the pantry. She always pulled it together before coming back out into the kitchen. I knew she was hurting, too. She had been with Jack for six years; he was a saving grace for her. She was able to send money to her family who still lived in the Philippines.

I was finishing placing a few things around the table when Sumiko told me that Jack wanted me upstairs. I hurried up to see what he needed.

He was out of bed and sitting in the window seat. He motioned for me to join him.

As I sat down, he took my hand, "Hello, beautiful."

"Hi," I said.

He handed me a wrapped gift box. "Happy 8 month Anniversary, my love."

I took the gift in my hands and untied the blue bow that surrounded it. Something from Tiffany's was waiting for me inside the box. I opened the box to find the most beautiful pendant with a two-carat diamond in the middle and sapphires surrounding it in a circle.

I gasped. "Jack! It's beautiful. Thank you, thank you."

He smiled. "Here, let me put it on you."

He attached the clasp. I stood up to look at it in the mirror. Tears came to my eyes. I walked back over to him and hugged and kissed him.

I stood up and helped him stand, too. He put his arm in mine, and we walked downstairs. We walked out to the patio. The whole family had arrived and was waiting for us. This time, Jack had tears in his eyes because he didn't know everyone was coming to dinner.

He kissed my cheek. "A wonderful gift. Thank you."

We all sat down and enjoyed a nice evening under the stars. The conversation was great with a lot of laughing. It was just what both of us needed: a respite from the sadness looming in our house. Jack had a nice time but was thoroughly exhausted by the end of the night. I helped him into bed and went back downstairs to say goodnight to our family. Then and only then were tears shed. They didn't know if it was the last time to spend with Jack. Tommy was not doing well. It was a lot for a nine-year-old to take in. Mom had him in counseling so he could talk to someone about death and how to handle the process. I think I needed it, too.

We crawled into bed, and I snuggled in beside Jack and fell asleep. During the night, I awoke to Jack wheezing. He was having difficulty breathing so I called an ambulance. By the time we arrived to the hospital, he was sedated and calm. After his doctor examined him, he asked me to step outside with him.

"Olivia, I'm sorry but I think this is the end. The cancer has taken over Jack's body and even entered his brain. He signed forms that we keep him comfortable at this point but not to do anything to keep him alive. I have given him a dose of morphine. I'm not sure if he'll wake up now."

I thanked the doctor and walked back inside the room to sit next to Jack. Jack's dad and brother came along with my parents. I called Sumiko around five to let her know. She showed up close to six with swollen eyes. We all gathered around his hospital bed in disbelief that Jack was actually leaving us. I placed his hand in mine and kissed him gently on the forehead. He opened his eyes a little.

"Jack, I love you. It's okay. We are all here. You can go now. I know you're in pain. Let go. We love you so much." I started crying.

He looked at me one more time, smiled, and closed his eyes. The machine made that horrible sound. The sound of no more life. A long beep that still rings in my ears.

I was amazed at how many people came to the funeral. I wore Jack's favorite green dress. He made me promise not to wear black. I sat there in front of his coffin. I just kept staring like maybe if I stared hard enough, he would pop open the lid and jump out.

The service was over and most people had left. I couldn't get myself to leave. I could see my parents standing in the distance giving me some space. Beautiful leaves were falling from the branch that reached over Jack's coffin. Knowing how much Jack loved fall, I was comforted knowing that each year the leaves would float down to rest on his space. I stood up, placed one hand on the coffin and the other on my growing stomach. Tears were running down my cheeks. I felt someone come up beside me and slip an arm around my waist. I looked over. It was Alex.

ACKNOWLEDGMENTS

I would like to thank my friends and family for the constant support during the time I wrote this novel. I would like to specifically thank my mom, Pam Akers, for her tireless editing and constant encouragement. Thank you to Erina Ruggeri for her help in the design of the cover and back of the novel. Lastly, thank you to some of my students and colleagues who were brave enough to read the novel and give helpful feedback.

Instagram
@ Erika Akers-Morse